EYE OF THE STORM

When Nadine Middleton travels to Egypt, she does not expect to meet Lancaster Smith, the man who discredited her father. As she embarks on a quest to clear Raleigh Middleton's name, she wonders who is friend and who is foe amongst the other passengers on the Nile steamer. With one apparent death and another person going missing, along with some mind-blowing and life-threatening riddles to solve, Nadine finds herself relying on Lancaster more and more — but can she trust him?

SALLY QUILFORD

EYE OF
THE STORM

Complete and Unabridged

LINFORD
Leicester

First published in Great Britain in 2016

First Linford Edition
published 2017

*A catalogue record for this book is available
from the British Library.*

ISBN 978–1–4448–3128–3

Published by
F. A. Thorpe (Publishing)
Anstey, Leicestershire

Set by Words & Graphics Ltd.
Anstey, Leicestershire
Printed and bound in Great Britain by
T. J. International Ltd., Padstow, Cornwall

This book is printed on acid-free paper

1

Dear Aunt Clementine,

I'm in Egypt at last! It is a place I have heard much about but never seen. The country is everything I imagined and more. It is a place of startling contrasts. The wonderful, talkative people in their native clothes; the stiff-upper-lipped English, who could just as well be off to an afternoon at Lord's; the aroma of food in the markets; the imams calling the faithful to prayer; the monuments almost as old as time; the pedlars; the beggars; the heat; the flies (I must admit I could do without them); and the sand that shifts with each breath of wind. All go to make up a country in which the scenery is ever-changing, yet at the same time eternal.

To think that just a few weeks

ago I was typing in a poky little office in London, and wondering if I could manage to find a coin for the electric meter to warm a can of soup when I returned to my bedsit. Now I am Personal Assistant to a Countess, and travelling in luxury!

I cannot tell you how grateful I am to you for finding me a place as Countess Chlomsky's companion. You said that if I helped you, you would help me.

As you have asked me to write to you regularly and to tell the truth about everyone and everything, I suppose I had better start with my new employer. Are you sure you want me to be honest about her?

Perhaps I should lie and tell you that she's an absolute dear, and easy to get along with. No? Oh, well. In that case, she can be rather difficult — as I found during my interview. That took place in London, just before we left. It was at her husband's embassy. Count Chlomsky is a diplomat for one of those Eastern European countries that is apparently going to play a major role in the coming war. But there are also rumours that he is a double agent. I have yet to decide if he is on our side or theirs.

I should say that he is rather a dear. He is completely devoted to his more domineering wife. He is a tiny little man, height-wise, but very round, having very much enjoyed the luxury dinners at his club. He has one of those Edward VII beards, and an almost courtly air. Despite his grand title, he never makes one feel like a servant. It is a trait that I have found only in the truly noble.

I appear to be procrastinating, don't I? Oh well, on to Countess Chlomsky. I'm sorry, Aunt Clementine, as she is your friend (as she is fond of telling everyone she meets). I gather you knew her as

Mrs Oakengate, a celebrated (she says) actress.

'And you are?' the countess asked, looking at me over a pair of spectacles. She was dressed in the fashion of the turn of the century, which I gather was her heyday.

'I am Nadine Middleton. My Aunt Clementine recommended me to you.'

'Ah yes, dear Clementine. I have not seen her for some years, but she is a very busy woman. You will know then that I was formerly Victoria Oakengate,' she said, with the air of an announcement.

I fell silent, not quite sure how to respond to her statement. She appeared to want me to be impressed. 'I see,' was all I managed.

'The actress?'

'Oh . . . '

'Goodness, how old are you?'

'I'm twenty-three. But I'm told I'm very mature for my age.'

'And you've never heard of me?'

4

'I'm afraid not. Will I have seen any of your films?'

'Films? Films?' She said it with the air of Lady Bracknell discussing handbags. 'I did not appear in films. I was on the stage, child. The stage! My Juliet made Edward the seventh weep.'

'I'm afraid I don't get to the theatre very often.' I did not want to explain to her that it was cheaper to go to the pictures than it was to go to the theatre. Plus, one did not have to dress up for the pictures. 'I'm sure I wish I had seen you in the theatre, but it was probably before I was born.'

I knew the moment I said it that it was not the right thing to say. 'I mean that I don't know how long you've been married, and that it's probably been a while since you acted and that I am sorry to have missed the chance to see you perform.' I ran out of breath by the last word, so it came out as a gasp. I want to assure you, Aunt Clementine, that I am not a girl who becomes breathless at regular intervals.

That is just the effect the countess had on me.

'I am not at all sure about you,' the countess said. 'My other girls were far more suited to the role. More docile. All my girls married well, you know.'

'Did they?'

'Oh yes. One married a top-ranking secret agent, and the last girl I had — prior to my marriage — married a prince.'

'How exciting!' Personally I could not think of anything more boring than marrying a stuffy old prince. None of those I'd seen, barring Edward VIII, were that attractive.

'You're pretty enough . . . ' She looked me up and down in a way that was not quite complimentary. I am ashamed to say that I was not looking my best. My stockings had been darned too often, and my suit, which had once been a deep dark blue, was becoming grey with age. ' . . . in your way,' she continued. 'We would have to buy you new clothes, of course. Perhaps cut your hair. It is hardly fashionable.'

'The truth is, Countess Chlomsky, things have been difficult since my father went missing five years ago. It is too soon to declare him dead, and so I am unable to claim my inheritance, such as it is.'

'How tragic,' she said. I would like to say she softened, but she seemed to enjoy my plight rather too much for that. 'And who was your father?'

'He was the archaeologist Raleigh Middleton.'

'Is that the man who was discredited and then went missing?' The countess's eyes gleamed.

'That's absolute balderdash,' I said, again without thinking. Considering how much I wanted to get to Egypt, I was not doing a very good job of getting myself there. 'What I mean is that the people who started that rumour were talking absolute balderdash. My father was not discredited. Or rather he was, but it was unjust. He was betrayed by someone who claimed to be a friend.'

'But his findings were found to be dubious, according to some of the best minds in the land.' I guessed that by 'the land' she meant England. It would not occur to the countess that there is a whole world of scientists out there.

'Yes, that is true.'

'And he himself was sure that this jewel — what was it called? — The Eye of the Storm? That this jewel had magical properties?' Despite her hesitation, I suspected that she knew exactly what she was talking about. She had investigated me before my arrival. I supposed that was fair, but it also meant she had already made up her mind about me, which was not so good.

'Yes.' I hung my head. It had been my father's obsession. I was still in secretarial college when he went in search of it and I had not seen him since. Word had come that he had died, but it was not proof enough for the family solicitors.

'It must be difficult for you, being his

daughter, living with the shame of his stupidity.'

I wanted to tell her that, no, it was not difficult at all. I loved Dad, despite his obsessions. He was — is — one of England's true eccentrics, and it is hard not to love him.

Instead, I gauged her reaction, and decided upon a rather wan, 'Life has not been easy.' I was not exactly lying. Life has been difficult since Dad went missing, especially now Mum isn't here anymore, but I am no victim and I will not allow the countess to turn me into one.

'Poor child. Yes, you must come with me. You would not be my first companion to have a tragic background. One girl's father was hanged as a traitor, and another had a mother and a father who both betrayed their country.' She spoke proudly. 'I think you and I will rub along together nicely, Nadine.'

The next thing I knew, the countess called in a dressmaker, who fitted me out with new clothes: a sand-coloured skirt suit for the daytime, with a couple of white blouses that I could alternate; new stockings and underwear; and two very pretty gossamer evening dresses. Nothing too flashy, but I did not mind that. I am, after all, a mere companion, and I was grateful for the new garments. I know I should be more grateful to the countess. And I am, really. But somehow my gratitude was tinged with bitterness when she insisted on introducing me to the dressmaker, and everyone else for that matter, as 'The daughter of the discredited archaeologist, Raleigh Middleton'.

Honestly, Aunt Clementine, I very nearly told her where to stick her new clothes. But I remembered our deal and I promise I will keep to it, even if it does mean gritting my teeth until they hurt.

So that I didn't feel completely beholden to her for my clothing, I also took a couple of pairs of Dad's khaki shorts, as I felt they might come in handy if the going got a bit rough. I added two white shirts, a tan leather waistcoat that was crinkled with age, and a white Fedora. Well, it had been white once. Time and the sweat of Dad's brow had left it a rather dingy grey, but I didn't mind. It reminded me of him. I had to take in the shorts and shirts, and even then they were quite voluminous — Dad did love his treacle pudding, even in the desert — but I figured that would be better in the extreme heat of North Africa.

My long fair hair has been cut into a shoulder-length bob. It was a wrench to see all that hair falling to the floor, but I think the shorter style suits me. New hairdo, new life.

I have just unpacked at the hotel in Alexandria. As you know, we are travelling down the Nile tomorrow. But tonight we are going to an ex-pat club for a dinner dance. I will complete this letter when I return.

★ ★ ★

It is morning and in a few hours we will catch the train from Ramses Station to Cairo, in order to join our cruise, but I will tell you something of our evening out as there were some interesting conversations and events.

Sadly, it seems the English are not so welcome here. The locals resent our occupancy, and sometimes with good reason. Some of the ex-pats living here treat the place like it still belongs to the empire. When you walk into the English club, you could be walking into any old boys' club in Britain, which rather dampened my initial enthusiasm for being in Egypt. The only difference is the heat and the native waiting staff, who work quietly and efficiently to ensure all our needs are met.

The British residents give every impression of acting as if they are still in Brighton or at Henley. There is roast beef and Yorkshire pudding on the menu, and Pimms at the bar. The ex-pats seem to make no attempt to assimilate into the community. They are content in their superiority and treat the Egyptians accordingly. It is no wonder we are not welcome.

The presence of the Royal Navy base in Alexandria does nothing to assuage the locals. I was invited there by a handsome young subaltern, but I had to decline as we are leaving this morning. I am not sure I could tell you anything you don't know about the base anyway.

Now to our fellow passengers. The idea of the dinner dance was to meet them. I can only give you a sketch of them at the moment, Aunt Clementine, but I will report back when I have had time to make a better judgement.

Countess Chlomsky was rather put out that her own superiority was usurped by that of a certain Prince Ari. He is a very handsome Nubian man of around forty years old, with olive skin and black hair, slightly greying at the temples. He has the dazzling white smile of a film star, and he smiles a lot.

He is joining the Nile cruise on some sort of diplomatic mission, though what relation he is to the Egyptian royal family, I do not know. Count Chlomsky tells me that there are lots of princes in this part of the world as the dynasty has many branches. Prince Ari treated me graciously, considering the countess kept dropping outrageous hints about us marrying!

'I was telling dear Nadine that all my girls marry well,' she told him. 'And now I have introduced her to you, I am sure you will do very nicely for her.'

'I, erm . . . I am not looking for a husband,' I told the prince. I almost said that if I was, he would definitely be on the list; but thankfully I held my tongue for once.

He smiled and said, 'And I do not seek a wife. But if I am ever in the market, I assure you I will bear you in mind.' He spoke with an English public school accent, and I gather he attended both Eton and Cambridge before joining our army. 'It is the best in the world,' he told us, 'and I want to be the best.'

Also on our trip will be a Miss Gloria Sutton and her brother, Charles. They are in their early twenties, like me. She is very tall and slender, with auburn hair. He is a couple of inches shorter than his sister, with lank blond hair. He's good looking in his way, but very quiet and a little bit shy, I think. 'We wanted to see Egypt before the war started,' Miss Sutton told me. 'I'm sure we won't be able to leave England very much afterwards.'

Talk of the impending war is everywhere. No one really expects 'peace in our time', yet at the moment we all seem to be in limbo. It is the calm before the storm . . .

'Has your brother not enlisted?' I asked. At the time, Charles Sutton was dancing with a young schoolteacher who will also be joining us.

'Charles? Oh, goodness no. He is not well enough to fight.' Miss Sutton did not go into specifics.

He did not seem to be having much trouble doing the foxtrot with the schoolteacher.

His partner's name was Miss Valerie Bentley, who I take to be around twenty-eight years of age. She is every inch the schoolmarm, with her hair pulled back in a tight bun, and wearing a severe grey dress that seemed much too hot for the climate, but perhaps like me she is not very well-off. She has not spoken to me much — the countess quickly dismissed the Bentley family as 'trade', and none too quietly either — but Miss Bentley has a warm smile and I can see how children would be drawn to her.

Our final fellow passenger is Cyrus Hardcastle, the arms manufacturer. You must know him. He tells us he is in Egypt on business.

'But I thought to myself, 'Why not take the Nile cruise, Cyrus?'' he told me as we dined. 'I'm a self-made man, Miss Middleton. Not much time for holidays in my youth. Oh, no. A trip to the seaside and a bag of chips was about all we could afford. And even then only when we had time. I went into the factory when I was twelve. Twenty years later, I bought it off the owner, and for the last twenty years it's been mine. But I've never had a good holiday so it's about time I did. I might be in the market for a wife too.' He winked at me then looked at the countess expectantly as she passed by in the arms of her husband.

'Hmm,' was all she said, which I was rather relieved about. Mr Hardcastle seems a decent enough man. One of those salt-of-the-earth types. But not exactly what I'm looking for in a husband. I would much rather marry the prince if I have to. Goodness that must sound very snobbish of me. It is not a matter of class, but merely of taste. Mr Hardcastle has hair pulled across his head, in what I believe they call a comb-over, and rather fat, soggy-looking lips. The prince, with his head of thick black curls and sensual mouth, suffers from neither of those afflictions.

Anyway, Mr Hardcastle asked me to dance with him again, and as I could not really refuse, we took to the floor for a waltz. I must admit I was relieved it was not a tango.

'You're Middleton's daughter,' he informed me whilst we danced, as if I had no knowledge of the matter. I could not answer to begin with, as I had to hastily move one of my feet from beneath his size thirteen loafers.

'Yes, that is correct.'

'Good man. Good man. Pity about them discrediting him the way they did. I believe that all men should be free to dream, Miss Middleton. Even if those dreams may seem far-reaching to some. How else would we have had tanks in the Great War, and now have the means for battles in the air for this one coming? I daresay your father shared his work with you all the time.'

'Not exactly,' I said, trying to keep step. Mr Hardcastle had already crushed my toes twice. 'My mother and father were separated when I was a child. I only saw him occasionally. He used to come to my school and take me out to lunch at the Lyon's Corner House.'

'But he must have told you something of his work.'

'In the few fleeting moments we had, we talked of other things.' To be honest, I cannot remember much of what my father and I talked about during our meetings. I rather think we said very little. He knew nothing of my life and of his I only knew what I read in the papers. As a child, in awe of this big booming man, I was too shy to ask him if any of it was the truth.

'Such as what?' He barked out the question, making me feel that I was being interrogated.

'My education,' I said quickly, remembering one conversation. 'Dad wanted me to go to university and study archaeology, but Mum wouldn't hear of it. She said that she had lost my father to his subject, and she was determined not to lose me. Then she died anyway, not long after Dad went missing.'

Most people would have answered that with regrets for my mother's loss. Not so Mr Hardcastle. 'So he never told you about this, erm . . . 'Eye of the Storm'?'

'I've heard of it, of course. But I have no personal knowledge of it.'

I hope, Aunt Clementine, that you understand why I lied to Mr Hardcastle. He was not the first person to have quizzed me about the jewel, as you know. And after my bedsit was broken into and ransacked, just before I left for Egypt, I felt I had to be careful. You are the only one I can trust.

When the dance ended (much to the relief of my feet!), we went back to the table, but Mr Hardcastle would not shut up about the jewel.

'Ah, yes, the Eye of the Storm,' said Prince Ari, in his liquid tones. (I admit I was rather taken with him, but I was not going to allow the countess to make my future for me.) 'They say that he who owns it can see all of creation from beginning to end.'

'Why is it called the Eye of the Storm?' asked the countess.

'Those who stand in the vicinity of the jewel, when it is activated, are as if they are standing in the eye of a storm. A safe haven. For that is what creation is: a violent and destructive storm from beginning to end, with only a few calm moments to allow us to catch our breath.'

'I hope life is better than that,' I said. 'True there have been wars, but for the most part we muddle along, don't we?' I realised I was being naïve, but I refuse to think that our world is beyond hope.

The prince fixed me with his gaze. 'Do we, as you say, *muddle along*, Miss Middleton? It is but twenty-one years since the world was last at war, and now we are on the brink of another conflict. Already Hitler is causing chaos in Germany and Austria. Soon he will march into Poland. You mark my words. And this has the capacity to be even worse than the Great War.' He looked at Mr Hardcastle, and I got the distinct impression he did not like him. 'The arms manufacturers have seen to that. And now there is a talk of a bomb that will end all wars, and probably end us all in the process.'

'Now then, Prince,' Mr Hardcastle said. 'You'll be glad of us arms dealers if there is a big war and you have to defend your family.'

The prince nodded. 'I concede that point, Mr Hardcastle. But how much better would the world be without weapons?'

'You're a pacifist,' Miss Bentley said to the prince.

'Is that a bad thing, Miss Bentley?'

'No, not at all. It makes a nice change from all this talk of war.'

'I hope, Your Highness,' said the countess, 'that you will do your duty if and when there is a war.'

'My duty to whom, Countess?'

'Well . . . to the right side of course.'

'What is the right side?' I sensed the prince was being deliberately provocative. He looked at me, and I'm sure I saw him wink.

The countess looked shocked. 'You surely cannot mean Hitler . . . Oh . . . ' She noticed, as we all did, that the prince's eyes twinkled. 'You're teasing me.'

'It is not so certain that everyone will think that way,' said her husband. Count Chlomsky had been quiet until then. 'King Farouk does not particularly welcome the British. Do you think he can be trusted if there is a war, Prince Ari?'

'I would be a traitor to say otherwise,' said Prince Ari with a courteous nod of his head.

'I hear that he insists on six hundred oysters a week whilst his many people starve,' Miss Bentley said. Her eyes flashed angrily. 'Not to mention his hundreds of cars. Really, how many cars can one man need?'

'He is still a young man,' the count said mildly. 'Remember that he was only sixteen when he took the throne three years ago. Any young man coming to power is bound to want to enjoy the benefits of those powers.'

I guessed that the count was being diplomatic for Prince Ari's sake. I did wonder if we could get into trouble for discussing the king so openly. That was the thing about being in a British club. One truly felt one was in Britain, with all the security that engendered. The count's words reminded us all that we had to be more careful. The club was not like the Embassy, which was classed as British soil.

Look at the time. I must go to the station. I will have to post this letter from Cairo. I may not be able to write as often once we're on the boat, but I will send reports whenever I can.

Your loving niece,
Nadine Middleton
P.S. My hands tremble as I write this. Did you know about him? Or will it be

as much of a surprise to you as it is to me?

I suppose I should explain why I am so fraught.

We caught the train at Ramses Station. The count had booked us sleeping carriages, even though we are not travelling that far. It at least gave us somewhere private to rest. But I could not settle in the heat. I went out into the corridor and opened a window above the exit door to get some fresh air. Miss Bentley was there too. We struck up a conversation. I said she could call me Nadine, and she said I could call her Valerie. I told her of my work with the countess, she told me of the international school she had just left and how she was now going on to work with a British family.

'I'll miss the children at the school, but with only two children to teach, I'll have much more free time,' she explained.

We were some miles out of Alexandria and moving into the desert when a cloud of dust appeared in the distance behind us.

'What is that?' I asked.

'I don't know,' said Valerie. 'Is it a car?'

The movement seemed wrong for a car, but with the heat causing everything to appear as a mirage, it took a while for the image to become clear. 'It's a horse and rider!' I said. 'I think he's trying to catch up with the train.' As it drew nearer, I saw that its rider was dressed in Arab garb, his face covered against the rising sand.

The horse was magnificent; a white Arab stallion. With the rider all dressed in white, his muscles straining against the linen, the effect was that of an avenging angel, bearing down on us. I felt sure he would fail, but in no time at all, he was neck and neck with the door by which I stood. The thunder of hooves competed with the engine of the train to deafen us.

'Open the goddamn door!' the rider

cried, in English but with an American accent.

Completely surprised, I did as he asked. First he threw a long bedroll, then a haversack, then, to our amazement, he hurled himself from the horse and onto the side of the train, letting the horse ride off into the desert alone. He clung to the door, as it swung perilously outwards. He clung on with one hand, and I grabbed the other, pulling him in. The door swung back in again and he was able to land in the corridor. I pulled the door shut with a bang.

I looked out at the horse, wondering what might happen to him.

'Don't worry,' said the man. 'He can find his way back home well enough.'

I realised then that I knew the voice, but I was so shocked by his arrival, I could barely speak. He took the headgear from around his face, and then I saw him properly, his steel grey eyes and that crooked smile I knew so well, looking down at me from six feet four inches.

'Hi, Nadine,' he said. 'How you doing? It's been a long time.'

'Lancaster Smith . . . ' I murmured, needing to put a name to the devil that stood before me. For to me he was no avenging angel.

Did you know that he was going to be here, Aunt Clementine? Did you know that, five years after ruining our lives, Professor Lancaster Smith was once again going to come into my world and turn it upside-down?

2

'All my girls married well.'

Countess Chlomsky held forth on her favourite subject as the assorted travellers met in the restaurant car for afternoon tea. Nadine Middleton, simmering silently and trying hard not to glare at Lancaster Smith, wrote an address on an envelope and sealed it. She would have to post it when they got to Cairo.

The overhead fans did little to cool the carriage, and the Earl Grey tea only made Nadine feel hotter. Or perhaps, she thought, that was the proximity of Lance. She shuddered at how easily that diminutive came to mind. Only his closest friends called him Lance, and she was no longer that.

'I intend to see if I can find Nadine a grand husband.' The countess fixed her eyes on Prince Ari, who politely smiled and turned his handsome head to look out of the window.

'I do not want a grand husband,' Nadine said under her breath. She forced a smile. 'But I thank you for your interest, Countess.'

'Oh, but you will marry well, dear,' said the countess. 'Tell her, Count. Tell her how well my other girls did.' The countess never addressed her husband by his first name. In fact, Nadine was not even sure what it was.

'I think you have already told us, Victoria,' the count said mildly. 'But perhaps it is best to let these things happen naturally, dear.'

'Oh, of course. I will not interfere one little bit. But there is nothing wrong in pushing the girl in the right direction. What of you, Mr Smith? What are your credentials?'

'I'm no prince,' said Lance. 'I'm a professor of archaeology and, I fear, much too lowly for your purposes.'

'Thank heaven for small mercies,' Nadine said in mock-sweet tones.

'I see you have not lost your scorpion sting.' Lance's lips curved into the lopsided grin she knew so well. Why was it, she wondered, that his presence could unnerve her so much, yet he acted as if nothing was amiss between them?

'The newspapers call you the cowboy professor,' said Miss Sutton. She and her brother were seated near the back of the carriage, having come in later than everyone else. 'My brother, Charles and I are great fans of your exploits.'

Lance nodded his thanks. 'I must confess that many are exaggerated.'

'And not just by the newspapers,' said Nadine.

'Is it true that you once found Moses' staff?' asked Valerie Bentley. 'And that it has the power to heal?'

Lance laughed. 'No wooden object would survive that long,' he said. 'It's all foolish nonsense made up by the newspapers who are bored with Egyptian mummies and Sarcophaguses. No offence, Prince Ari.'

'None taken,' said the prince. 'Your archaeologists have sacked our country for so long, it is not surprising that they were bored with their finds.'

'Touché,' Lance grinned.

'That told you,' said Nadine.

'Nadine, go and fetch my shawl,' the countess commanded. She cast Nadine a warning glance. Leaning over, she said quietly, 'Please remember that you are my companion and that your behaviour therefore reflects upon me.'

'Yes, countess. I'm very sorry.' Nadine coloured up. She had forgotten her real reason for being there. In fact, even the countess would be surprised at her real purpose, but she knew that she had to play the game, at least as far as the Second Cataract. That was days away. Nadine feared she could not be civil to Lance for that long, not even for the sake of keeping her job.

Then it occurred to her that she might not have to. For all she knew, he was only going as far as Cairo. She wished she could find out, without appearing to show too much interest in him. She did not want to give him any encouragement. Not after what he had done.

She got up and walked unsteadily to the sleeping carriages. It was just her luck that, as she became level with Lance, the train gave a jolt and she stumbled. He caught her in his outstretched arms, and she felt sure the heat from him would sear a hole in her sleeve.

'Thank you,' she said, awkwardly righting herself.

'You're welcome,' he said. 'And in case you're wondering, I'm joining the cruise to the Second Cataract.'

'Why?' She stopped in her tracks. 'Surely such a cruise would be boring for an adventurer like you.'

'Oh, I don't know. I think this one might be particularly interesting.'

Aware that everyone was watching, Nadine went about her business. She found the countess's scarf and then went to her own carriage in order to give herself time to cool down and face Lance on more certain footing. If that were at all possible.

She unlocked her door to find that the small carriage had been completely ransacked. The contents of her suitcase were strewn all over the floor. The cushions on the seat-cum-bed had been pulled up, and the empty spaces underneath searched. There was a small corner compartment in the carriage inside which was a vanity unit, including a sink. That too had been opened, and her wash bag torn apart.

'Dear God . . . ' she murmured.

'What's happened?' said a familiar deep voice behind her.

'Go away, Lance. I don't need your help.'

'No I won't. And you do. I'm guessing this wasn't a common or garden burglar.'

She turned to face him. 'Nothing is missing as far as I can see. I don't have much of value anyway.'

'What were they looking for?'

'How should I know?'

He looked at her for a long time, as if waiting for her to tell him the truth.

'The last time someone looked at me like that was my headmistress at boarding school, and she didn't get anything out of me either,' she told him.

'Let me tell you what I think.'

'Oh, please do. I always await your pronouncements with bated breath.'

'Your father kept a journal of his findings. He was never without it. It was rumoured that the journal showed the hiding place of the Eye of the Storm. When he went missing, he left everything he owned in his tent in the desert. The journal was not amongst his things then, and has never been found. A lot of people would like to get their hands on it.'

'Including you? Oh no, wait. You wouldn't be interested, because you publicly denounced my father as a fantasist and a liar.'

'It was the hardest thing I ever had to do, Nadine.'

'I'm sure you cried all the way to the bank after the newspaper paid you for your article slandering Raleigh Middleton.'

'I wasn't paid for it.'

'No?'

'No.'

'That somehow makes it worse, Lance. He was your mentor. He treated you like a son, as did my mother. I . . .' She just stopped herself from admitting her own feelings on the matter. 'I don't know how you could do that to him.'

'I had my reasons. Just as I have my reasons for being here. You should go home, Nadine. It isn't safe for you to be in Egypt. There are dark forces at work here.'

'I thought you didn't believe in all that mumbo-jumbo.'

'You don't have to believe in the supernatural to know that true evil is more than possible amongst real live human beings. That's what I'm talking

36

about. The evil that men do. The evil that men *will* do in order to gain power.'

'If the Eye of the Storm is without supernatural power, then I don't know what you're worried about.'

'I'm worried that you'll be harmed. If you believe that finding that stone will clear your father's name, then let me tell you that it isn't worth the risk you're taking.'

'You're mistaken, Lance. I'm here merely as a companion to the countess. Which reminds me, I must return to her.'

'And all the letters to dear Aunt Clementine?'

Nadine felt her face redden. 'She's been very good to me, and I promised to tell her of my trip.'

Lance smiled. 'I'll bet you did. Do I get a mention?'

'No, I hardly thought you worth mentioning at all.'

That made him laugh. 'This . . . ' He pointed to her, then to himself.

' . . . this animosity isn't about your father at all, is it? It's because of what happened between us.'

'Oh, believe me, Lance, I've been rejected by much more interesting men since.' That did not come out quite how Nadine meant it to. 'You were absolutely right. I was only seventeen years old, and you were . . . are . . . too old for me. In fact, I'd say I had a lucky escape.'

As she left the carriage and shut the door, her hands were shaking. She hoped he would not notice how the memory affected her. She had been seventeen, and Lance twenty-five at the time. They were at a dance thrown by the dean of the university, and she had flirted outrageously with Lance. At first, he had taken it with good humour. But later in the evening, when they were in the garden and she tried to kiss him, he had pushed her away.

'I'm not interested in you in that way,' he had said, his normally amused expression becoming cold and hard.

'I love you, Lance,' she had said. 'I've loved you forever.'

'Well, don't love me. Or at least come back when you're a grown-up.'

She went to kiss him again, but he had turned and walked away from her, leaving her feeling foolish. She told herself that she hated him then, but deep down she knew that was not true. It was not long after that night that he discredited her father, and then she really did hate him. Or so she kept telling herself.

The other travellers were horrified to hear that Nadine's carriage had been ransacked.

'One can never trust foreigners,' Mr Hardcastle said. 'Thieves and cut-throats, the lot of them.'

'I don't believe that is true at all,' Nadine protested. Instead, she looked at her fellow passengers, and wondered which of them she could trust. Lance? It was noticeable that her sleeping car had been ransacked since his arrival. Perhaps he cared more about the stone than he wanted to admit. The countess? No, perhaps not, Nadine thought. Or, if she had, she would send someone else to do it for her. She did have a lady's maid called Claudette, but she had gone ahead to Cairo to ready the countess's suite. The count? Also possible, despite his mild demeanour. The prince? He was a possibility. Rich people usually wanted to be *very* rich. The brother and sister Sutton? They had come into the restaurant car later than everyone else. Miss Bentley? Nadine liked her too much to think badly of her — but who knew what dreams and desires a schoolmarm had? Mr Hardcastle? Or maybe his secretary, Devon, who had joined them on the train, having travelled straight from England. Devon was a taciturn young man of about twenty-seven, the polar opposite of his ebullient employer.

'Probably that old Arab sitting up on the roof,' Mr Hardcastle carried on regardless, treating the entire restaurant car to his opinion on foreigners and their deceitful ways. 'Think yourself lucky that your honour is still intact, Miss Middleton.'

Nadine began to wonder if the silly man protested too much . . .

There were others in the restaurant car, but they were not part of Nadine's party. That did not necessarily mean they didn't have some interest in finding her father's journal. If, indeed, that had been the true reason for the break-in . . .

Soon the train rolled into Cairo and they were once again outside in the blistering heat, overwhelmed by the pedlars and beggars who followed them all the way to the hotel: a neoclassical building that had once been a palace before changing hands and spending some time as a hospital. It had been refurbished to offer the sort of luxury only the very wealthy could afford.

They stepped out of the heat and into the cool foyer. Nadine looked around and was surprised to see that Valerie Bentley was still with them. She wondered how a simple schoolmarm could afford such a place, but could only assume it was part of the package arranged by Thomas Cook, who were also in charge of the Nile Cruise.

Nadine went to the desk to check in for the count and countess.

'Ah, Miss Middleton,' said the desk clerk, with a courteous bow. 'We have been holding a parcel for you.' He handed over the small parcel.

'Really? Thank you,' she said, taking it from him. She went to offer a tip, but the man refused.

'Please, no. It is a courtesy to our guests.'

'Thank you.'

She looked at the handwriting on the parcel, trying to gain some insight into who might have sent it to her. Judging by all the crossings-out on the front, it appeared to have followed her across Europe.

Turning away from the desk, she saw Lance watching her with interest. She instinctively held the parcel closer to her breast. She wondered if it was what she thought it was, or just something Aunt Clementine had sent. Either way, it was no one's business but hers.

It was a while before she could open it and find out. She had to settle the countess into her room. Although the maid had done most of the work, the countess needed Nadine to write letters and thank-you cards, and set up a typewriter.

'My memoirs are going to set the theatrical world alight,' the countess told her, not for the first time. 'And I am hoping that you will provide me with my postscript, Nadine. I already saw the way the prince looked at you.'

'I don't think he looked at me at all,' Nadine said politely.

'Now, dear girl, don't bother with false modesty. You're a pretty girl, and he's a handsome man. It's only right you should be together. If not him, then Mr Hardcastle.'

'What about Lancaster Smith?' Nadine asked, only half-teasing.

'Oh, the man is almost a savage. No, dear. That would do no good at all. You'd be living in tents in the desert for the rest of your life. At least when you weren't jumping onto trains. Don't think I don't know about his dramatic arrival. Really, why he can't catch the train like normal people, I don't know. Now, I'd like you to type up some of my notes before you change for dinner, and then I want you to post some letters and parcels for me before you go to bed. They're next to the typewriter. One is most important as it holds the latest chapters of the memoir for my agent.'

Nadine had no choice but to comply, despite longing to take a bath and wash away the sweat and grime of travel. She worked until late afternoon, and just about had time to bathe and dress before going down for dinner.

Dinner was a leisurely affair, and she was glad to see that the menu here was less English in flavour. She particularly enjoyed the *Macaronie Béchamel* and the freshly baked pita bread called *Eish Masri*. After months of worrying where the next meal would come from, Nadine could not help overeating.

'*Eish*,' the prince informed them, 'means 'a way of life'. Bread is a very important part of every Egyptian meal.'

'As it is where I come from,' Nadine quipped, remembering having to decide whether she could toast some for her evening meal back in England.

'Man cannot live by bread alone,' said Mr Hardcastle. 'Speaking for myself, I'd like some fish and chips and thickly spread butter to go with it.'

Everyone laughed, but it seemed clear from his complaints that Mr Hardcastle meant it. 'What's this?' he would ask as each dish was brought. Then he picked at it with his fork, sniffing the food before reluctantly eating it.

They finished with Baklava: sweet pastries that melted in the mouth. Mr Hardcastle didn't complain about those, and even asked for more.

After dinner, the count and countess said they were retiring. 'You are free for the rest of the evening, Nadine,' the countess told her. 'Perhaps the prince can show you the sights, but don't forget to post my letters.'

'I regret,' the prince said, bowing his head, 'that I have a prior engagement. Perhaps some other time?'

'Of course,' Nadine said, secretly relieved. She wanted to be alone to open her parcel.

'I will walk with you, Miss Middleton,' said Miss Sutton. 'I need to clear my head. Charles, it's time you went to bed.'

'Yes, dear,' her brother replied. He got up immediately and left.

Nadine did not feel she could refuse, so she and Miss Sutton went out into the town. Even though the sun was setting, there was a lot going on. The market was still open, so they browsed the stalls. There was a lot of tourist tat, as in most places, but also some very lovely bargains to be had on the stalls dedicated to the local residents.

'Tell me about Lancaster Smith,' Miss Sutton said as they walked. 'You've known him a long time?'

'Erm, yes, since I was about thirteen. He was my father's student for a while. He came over on a scholarship from Harvard.'

'Where is he from?'

'His family are from America, but I think his father was British. To be honest, he doesn't talk about them much. Why, do you like him?' The idea made Nadine feel miserable. She pushed the feeling aside and told herself it was none of her business if Miss Sutton fancied Lance.

'Oh, goodness no. I just wondered about him. He seemed to come from nowhere. Did he tell you what he was doing in Egypt?'

'No, he didn't. He doesn't really share his plans with me.'

'It's odd, him turning up here like this. I thought . . . ' Miss Sutton paused.

'Yes?'

'Oh, I'd read somewhere that he was already on a dig down near the Second Cataract. So it was a surprise to see him on the train from Alexandria. I wonder what he was doing there.'

'I'm afraid I can't help you with that.'

As they walked, Nadine realised that they had left the main town and had somehow wandered into the back streets. 'I think we should go back,' she said, starting to turn. 'I forgot to post my letters.' As she turned, she saw a man in the shadows behind them. There was something about the way he stood, smoking a cigarette and watching them, that unnerved her. She was about to walk back, but the end of the passageway became blocked by a donkey and cart. 'Let's go this way,' she said, taking hold of Miss Sutton's arm and leading her towards the other end of the road.

The area seemed to be deserted. None of the homes along the pathway were lit up and all the doors were tightly shut. 'I'm afraid we've got lost,' she said.

'Is that man following us?' asked Miss Sutton. 'Oh goodness, I do believe he is. Careful, Miss Middleton. He could be a white-slaver.'

'I'm sure he isn't . . . ' Nadine said, but was not sure. She quickened her step, but it seemed the more she walked, the longer the passageway seemed to stretch.

Finally they reached a tiny crossroads of sorts. 'This way,' she said, starting to run to the right, reasoning it would bring them out near to the hotel. Miss Sutton followed her, and it was not long before the heat made them both out of breath. Nadine felt sweat trickle down her back.

She heard a voice shouting at her, and when she looked back briefly, she saw there was more than one man following them.

'I don't like this,' said Miss Sutton. She clung to Nadine's hand as they ran along. 'I don't like it at all. I wish

Charles was here. He would take care of us.'

Nadine was too polite to say that she doubted it. Charles seemed to be something of a wimp.

They reached another crossroads and turned down that one. Nadine could see what appeared to be a main thoroughfare at the end. If they could get amongst the crowds, they should be alright. They might even be able to jump into a taxi.

The men were closing in on them. Just before the women reached the end of the passageway, Miss Sutton tripped and went sprawling to the ground. Nadine cried out as one of the men caught her around the waist. She was manhandled against the wall, and the man searched her.

As it all took place, she tried to remember what the men looked like. The one who appeared to be in charge — and who was searching her in a very intrusive way — was not an Egyptian. He had blond hair and blue eyes. He reminded her of someone, but she could not place him. Finally, he found the parcel in her handbag and took it from her. He nodded to the other men and they left.

'Dear God,' Miss Sutton cried as Nadine helped her up. 'What was that all about?'

'I've no idea,' Nadine said, although she had an idea. 'Come on, let's get back to the hotel.'

They were both so shaken that they took a taxi. There was a message for Nadine to call in and see the countess before she went to bed.

'What on earth . . . ' the countess exclaimed when Nadine entered the suite. The old woman was dressed in an ivory silk negligee. The count sat in a chair drinking cognac, wearing a red monogrammed dressing gown. He quickly got up and poured a glass of brandy for Nadine, who drank it down without thinking, almost choking on the strong liquor. 'What has happened?' asked the countess.

'I'm so sorry, countess.' Nadine coughed to clear her throat. 'But Miss Sutton and I were attacked in the street.'

'That is hardly a reason to be sorry,' said the count, kindly. He stood up. 'Please, sit down, Miss Middleton.'

'I'm sorry,' Nadine continued. She realised that she wanted to cry, but she managed to contain herself. She sat down and the count brought her another glass of cognac.

'Take your time,' said the count.'

'Countess, I'm so sorry, but they stole the parcel holding your chapters.'

'Goodness,' said the countess, her eyes gleaming. 'I told you they were explosive, did I not, Count?'

The count smiled benignly at his wife, but his eyes looked at Nadine rather more shrewdly. She avoided his gaze as much as she could.

When the count and countess satisfied themselves that she was calm enough, she went back to her room. She half expected it to have been ransacked. An elderly Arab sat near the lifts, but he appeared to be asleep, so anyone might have passed him. Unless he was actually alert — but she had her doubts about that.

As she went into her room, she looked at him again, and for a moment felt sure he was the same man who had been sitting on top of the train. She brushed the thought aside, reflecting that it was not really nice of her to think that one Arab looked pretty much like another.

The parcel — Nadine's original parcel — was where she had left it. The room had a safe, but anyone might have broken into that. She had not expected anyone to search the spaces under the bathtub, so she had pushed it right to the back. It took a wire coathanger to drag it back to her, but at last she had it.

The first address on the parcel was the family home in Derbyshire. Then her bedsit in London; several hotels across Europe, where she had stayed with the count and countess; and finally the hotel in Cairo.

Sitting on her bed, her body fatigued from the travelling and the shock of being assaulted, she finally opened it.

Inside was a brown leather-bound book. She recognised it immediately. It had been one of her father's battered journals. He had hundreds of them packed amongst the things she had removed from Derbyshire when her mother died. But this was the one he had been using the last time she saw him. He liked to keep an account of all his digs. She opened the journal and a letter fell out, addressed to her.

Dearest Nadine,

If you are reading this journal, then I'm afraid, my darling girl, that it means I am dead.

It is also possible that you know about the Eye of the Storm and that someone plans to send you to find it. I think I can even guess who. Whilst I am mocked in public, in private my findings are taking very seriously. Tell your employers that they are not the only ones in search of the jewel.

I give you this journal only so that you may keep it safe and out of the hands of those who would use it for bad works. That may not mean what you think it does. Trust no one, Nadine.

You might wonder why I did not destroy the journal. I thought of that, but I could not bring myself to do it. All I have learned in the past few years is in this book, and I cannot imagine burning it so that all is lost. I am weak, I know that, but in here lies proof that I am not the madman they believe me to be.

There are dark forces at work in Nazi Germany and they will stop at nothing to find the Eye of the Storm. The jewel has powers beyond our comprehension and they cannot be allowed to attain it. I am no more content to let our own countrymen find it. We cannot trust what such power would do even to the most noble of people.

As for the journal, perhaps you will have more strength than I. Burn it. Bury it. Do anything to destroy it, but whatever you do, don't let it get into the wrong hands.

Show my solicitors this letter, and they will free up my estate so that you and your mother need not worry about money.

I want you to be safe, my darling. I may not have been a great father or husband, but know that I loved you and your mother right up until the end.

I end by begging you not to go in search of the Eye of the Storm yourself.

All my love
Dad

'Oh Dad.' Nadine hugged the letter to

her chest. 'Mum's not there, Dad. She's gone.' Tears rolled down her cheeks. 'I've no one now . . . ' For a while she could not move as grief overwhelmed her.

It was true that the letter solved her problems. All she had to do was take it to the probate office and her father's money would be released. But it was not just about the money. Nadine hated that people mocked her father. *Punch* magazine carried cartoons showing him as a raving madman; Hollywood had even made a film depicting Raleigh Middleton as a bungling professor; and to make matters worse, he became the punchline of a thousand jokes beginning, 'Who broke the arms off the Venus de Milo?'; 'Who broke the nose off the Sphinx?'.

That was not how she remembered her dad. She remembered him as a tall, bear-like man with a ready smile, but with a thirst for knowledge that drove him away from them all the time. He would come home sometimes, but after a week or two, both Nadine and her mother could tell he was ready to leave again. He became restless, dispirited, until her mother would say, 'Whatever it is, Raleigh, go and find it.'

The last time her mother had said it, she had added, 'And this time, don't bother coming back.'

Despite that, Celine Middleton waited for Raleigh to return, but it appeared that he had taken her at her word. Nadine believed without question that her mother had died of a broken heart, waiting for the man who would never be entirely happy with his family, even if he did love them deep down.

It was because of this that she gave into her mother's wish that she did not go to university to study archaeology. That did not take away Nadine's own wanderlust, so instead of Egypt, she had moved to London, promising her mother she would return at weekends. City life soon took over, and the visits became fewer and further between, not least because the pittance she earned did not allow for regular travel to the north. She was too proud to ask her mother for help.

'We both broke her heart,' Nadine said to herself now as the tears kept falling. 'We both abandoned her.'

She flicked idly through the journal. Amongst her father's writings were pictures of various artefacts and maps. The pages blurred as her tears fell. There was too much for her to take in, and she knew she would have to get into a calmer state of mind to work out what it all meant.

She walked over to the window and stared unseeing across the rooftops of Cairo, out into the distance. Instead, she saw her mother's sad eyes, and her own confusion about a father who said he loved them but could never live with them long enough to become a proper family.

The pain of rejection and loss had to be worth it, somehow. Regardless of what her father said, she would go in search of the Eye of the Storm, and find out one way or another if it had the magical properties her father believed it to have.

Whether she handed the jewel over at the end was another matter. As with the prospect of destroying the journal, she would decide what to do when the time came. For now, she was determined to follow this adventure through to the end.

3

'Nadine?' Lance caught up with her as she was leaving the hotel. The count and countess had been invited to a morning reception at one of the consulates. As far as the countess was aware, Nadine was in her room retyping the lost chapters of the memoirs. When they returned, Nadine planned to lie and say that the ribbon on the typewriter had run out, and that she had had no choice but to go in search of a new one.

'Yes? What is it?'

'Someone told me that you were attacked last night. Is that true?'

'Someone stole the countess's manuscript from me. There's no real harm done.'

His grey eyes squinted in the sunlight. 'You weren't hurt?'

'No, they didn't hurt me. Now, if

you'll excuse me, I'm going on an excursion before we leave for the Nile steamer.'

'Where are you going?'

She did not want to tell him, but it felt churlish not to. 'Elephantine.'

'I see.' For a moment, she believed he really did see. Did he know what she might find there? And, if so, did that mean he was also interested in finding it?

Nadine had spent most of the morning reading her father's journal, and the island of Elephantine was the first stop on the quest to find the Eye of the Storm. 'I really must hurry,' she said, rushing away from him.

'Hang on, I'll come with you.'

'What?' She stopped and turned back to face him. 'Why?'

'I'll come with you. There's a very interesting museum on Elephantine and I know something of its history.'

'Yes, but . . . ' What could she say to him to stop him from accompanying her? She did not own the ferry or the island. 'Why would you want to be with me? It's not as if we're friends.'

'I wish we could be.'

'After what you did to my father?' Her father's caution to trust no-one rang in her head.

'Will you believe me when I said that I had no choice?'

'You keep saying that, but why? Why did you have no choice?' Nadine really wanted to be on her way. Even though she wore a hat, the sun beat down on her head and shoulders. By lunchtime she would be wilting in the sun, so she wanted to get to the island before that happened. The heat had a way of dampening her powers of thought, as if draining the energy from her mind.

'I can't explain.'

'Can't, or won't? Oh, I don't have time for this.' She turned and started walking. It was disconcerting when he caught up with her and kept up the same pace. It seemed he was travelling with her whether she wished it or not.

'You look as if you're dressed to go

digging,' he said as they reached the jetty.

Nadine had put on the white shirt, khaki shorts and boots, thinking that she might well have to get dirty. During the night she had created an inside pocket in the shirt tails, into which she put the journal. The shirt tails were then tucked into her shorts. She doubted it would fool anyone for long, but it seemed safer than leaving it in her room. She guessed that once the assailants from the previous evening realised they were reading the rather dull account of a romance with a government minister, they would search her room again.

'It's cooler than wearing my suit or dresses,' she said airily. 'Don't you think women should wear shorts?'

'I certainly think *you* should,' he said.

They got the jetty just in time to catch the boat. The first few minutes were taken up with paying their fares. They went to find a seat, and were turning the corner to go the starboard side when they bumped into Valerie Bentley.

'Hello, Valerie,' said Nadine. 'I didn't know you were doing this trip.'

Valerie blushed, as if caught in some escapade. 'I thought I might as well, since the steamer doesn't leave until this evening. I was just going in search of a drink. Why don't you come with me?'

There was a bar inside the boat, where tourists sat with long, cool drinks.

'I think I'd like to look at the scenery,' said Nadine.

'Yes, me too,' Lance agreed.

'Oh, very well.' Valerie looked down to the ground. She still gave the impression of a schoolgirl being caught misbehaving. 'I'll see you in a little while, I'm sure.'

'Yes, of course.'

Nadine and Lance carried on walking along the starboard side, hoping to find a place near to the front. There was another set of double doors, leading to the bar, and Nadine wondered why Valerie had not used those.

'Well, this is a surprise,' said a loud voice from the bar.

'Oh, Mr Hardcastle.' Nadine's heart sank. Had everyone decided to go to Elephantine? Devon sat next to his employer, taking notes about something.

'Mr and Miss Sutton are here too,' said Hardcastle, indicating his other companions. 'Come and join us.'

'No, thank you,' Nadine said. 'If I drink now, I shall be asleep by lunchtime.' She and Lance carried on towards the front of the boat.

'I can't believe it,' she murmured. 'I'll never be able to lie to the countess now. Or is she here too? Is there to be no privacy?'

'Would you like me to go?' Lance raised an eyebrow.

'I thought that was obvious from the moment we met at the hotel door,' she said in wry tones. They looked at each other, and somehow the tension between them evaporated and they burst out laughing.

'What is funny?' another familiar voice asked.

'Oh, it's Prince Ari . . . ' It was too much for Nadine. She turned to hold on to the rail, stifling the giggles that refused to subside. She realised that she was becoming hysterical.

'Have I said something amusing?' she heard the prince ask Lance.

'No, it's just that we didn't expect to see our fellow travellers on this trip, Your Highness.'

'No,' said the prince in more serious tones. 'I too am surprised.'

Nadine turned to look at him, and saw that his handsome brow was furrowed. 'We don't wish to intrude, Your Highness.'

'Please. I have no wish to advertise my status. Call me Ari. And I may call you Nadine and Lancaster?'

'Just Lance will do,' he said to the prince.

Nadine nodded her own agreement.

'I hear Elephantine is a fascinating island,' she commented, for want of something more interesting to say.

'Yes, indeed,' said the prince. 'It was said to be the dwelling place of Khnum, the ram-headed god of the cataracts. Khnum controlled the Nile from caves beneath the island. There is a temple on the island. Perhaps you will see it?'

'Oh, I hope so,' Nadine said. 'Do you know anything of the Nilometer?'

'Indeed,' said the prince. 'The one on the island is a particularly fine example. It has ninety steps leading to the river. You must let me show you it,' he added courteously.

Nadine mentally kicked herself. She wanted to go there alone, but the Eye of the Storm was dominating all her thoughts. The words burst from her tongue as if needing to make space for other things. 'I'm sure there will be enough to see in the museum,' she said, 'and I do not have much time.'

By the time they reached Elephantine, the tour group had come together so it was natural that they went up to the Aswan museum *en masse*. She feared she would never get away.

After half an hour looking at ancient relics and learning about the interesting Jewish community who had lived on the island in times gone by, Nadine mentioned that she was going in search of a powder room. The other tourists said they would meet her at a café overlooking the Nile. She had no intention of doing that. She told herself that it was not at all unusual for a group of tourists to become separated, and doubted she would even be missed.

Ensuring she was not followed, Nadine worked her way back through the museum and out through a side door into the blinding sunshine. The Nilometer was just below the museum, and it was easy enough to walk down there without being seen. She found the set of eighty steps at the top of a high stone wall. The steps lead down to a narrow tunnel, which in turn led to an archway looking out onto the Nile.

The arch was an inlet through which the Nile flowed and rose or fell. At the side of each step was a measuring stick, to indicate the depth.

Nadine sat on the top step and reached into the inner pocket for a scrap of paper she had quickly scribbled on that morning.

The search for the Eye of the Storm, it read, *is allied to the four cardinal virtues of Prudence, Justice, Temperance and Courage, as discussed in Plato's Republic. They were appropriated by Christianity, which had come to Nubia by the fourth century. The Eye of the Storm can only be attained by finding the keys which represent each one of the virtues. These keys were spread throughout the first and second cataracts. It has taken me many years, but I have now discovered where they are. Sadly, my attempt at finding the first key on the island of Elephantine was interrupted by the appearance of a German spy who also showed an interest in the Nilometer.*

There followed her father's account of his meeting with the spy and the fight that ensued, which ended with her father having to leave so that he did not give the location away to his competitor. At the end of the page was a code of some sort: *Mother reads on the way to heaven 16:16. Find the key and you will be set free.*

Was it some sort of Bible quote? But if it was, there would surely be a book name to go with it, like Genesis. Nadine shook her head. What if it were simpler than that?

She carefully counted sixteen steps downwards, and then looked around for a sign. Many hieroglyphics, and a bit of modern-day graffiti had been gouged into the walls. '*Mother . . .*' she muttered. She had not had a deeply religious upbringing, but she seemed to remember from school that Prudence was the mother of all virtues. There was nothing on the sixteenth step that she could see to fit with what she had read in the journal.

It occurred to her that if one were going to heaven, one would be going upwards. She walked down to the bottom of the Nilometer and instead counted upwards, till reaching the sixteenth step. Once again, there were lots of different objects cut into the stone. 'Reads . . . ' she murmured. 'Reads.' Of course, one read books or papers. She found it right next to the sixteenth inch on the ruler.

It was a scroll, which was one of the symbols of Prudence. She pressed it — and nothing happened.

'Oh, come on,' she groaned. She pressed again, this time harder, and felt something give. Only it was not a secret compartment on the wall.

The step underneath her began to slide back. She quickly jumped onto the one above it, but that slid back too, and much more quickly.

Before she could find purchase, the

ground gave way beneath her feet and she plunged into darkness . . .

4

Nadine landed heavily on what appeared to be a very smooth slope. The only light came from the aperture above her, and that soon faded as she slid further and further into the darkness. As smooth as the slope was, it still caught on her bare legs, leaving painful scratches. Her backside was already bruised from the hard landing.

It seemed as if she fell downward for hours, but she reasoned it was probably only minutes. Perhaps only seconds. Finally, she landed on something soft.

'Thank God,' she whispered. Until the something soft beneath her began to move and scuttle away from her and she realised there were thousands of rats. A cold chill ran down her spine, as if every one of the rats had crawled over her grave. She clamped her mouth shut, determined not to be a helpless woman and scream. Despite that, when she felt the nip of sharp teeth on her leg, she whimpered. 'Ugh. I hate rats!'

She pulled herself up. This was easier said than done when her hands kept touching wet fur. She realised that there was water underneath all the rats, and wondered if it had come in from the Nile or from the sewers. The aroma and the existence of the rats suggested the latter.

After a while, her eyes became more accustomed to the dark, and she was able to make out a source of light in the distance. She hoped it led to the way out, but she could not be sure. The fact she could breathe suggested that air got into the tunnel from somewhere, and not just where she had fallen from the steps.

Nadine followed the light until it became stronger. Eventually, the tunnel opened out into a large circular chamber which had a light source from somewhere, only Nadine could not work out where it came from. There was a stone walkway around the edges, but in the centre a big black pit descended into an abyss. Only a waist-high guard rail separated the walkway and the drop.

Above the circle were dozens and dozens of keys on chains, hanging from the ceiling. Some were near to the walkway, but others were right in the centre. It did not take much to guess that the key she wanted would not be the easiest to find.

'Find the key and you will be set free,' she said out loud. 'All right — so how do I do that?'

She walked around the edge of the circle several times, wondering how on earth she was supposed to guess which key was correct. 'Prudence,' she said out loud. 'The mother of all virtues. Foresight, sagacity. Wisdom, insight, knowledge. What? Am I supposed to know? Like some sort of fortune-teller? And what happens if I pull the wrong key? Thanks for being so cryptic, Dad.'

As she spoke, she was aware of

someone else entering the chamber from the same direction as her. It was the man who had accosted her the night before and tried to steal her father's journal. He could not have been much older than Nadine, yet he had an arrogance that came from feeling superior to just about everyone in the world. To make matters worse, he was holding a Luger pistol and pointing it in her direction.

'Which key is it, Fraulein?' he asked with a German accent.

'I have no idea,' Nadine replied.

'So you do not mind if I try.'

'Knock yourself out,' she said, pointedly.

He began to walk around the circle in a clockwise direction, so Nadine moved counterclockwise. She feared being thrown into the abyss if he came close enough.

'It will not be in the centre,' he said. 'Because no one can reach that far.'

'Someone must have,' Nadine said. 'Someone put them all there.' That gave her an idea, but she did not share it with him, and she was careful not to look up at the ceiling in order to verify her suspicion.

'The keys, they have symbols on them,' the German said.

'Do they? I hadn't noticed.' Nadine was not lying, and it irritated her that he knew more than she did.

'So, I think the key we want will hold the same symbol as the stone you pressed to get us here. A scroll. But there are so many. Help me to find it.' He cocked the gun at her.

'Why? Who are you working for?'

'I work for the glory of our Fuhrer. Who sent you?'

'My Aunt Clementine.' It did not have quite the same ring.

'Pfft,' he said. 'Look for the key and I will not shoot you.'

Nadine only obeyed because it gave her an excuse to check if her theory was true.

They searched in silence for about ten minutes, always careful never to walk close to each other, circling the pit from opposite directions. Maybe, she thought, he was just as afraid as she of being pushed into the abyss. She noticed there was a pulley system on the roof, similar to the washing lines that ran between windows in high-rise buildings. Every key on the outer perimeter was attached to one of those in the centre.

'Ah,' said the German, causing Nadine's heart to drop. He too had realised it. 'So if I find . . . ' He clamped his lips shut. 'Wait!' he commanded. 'You will touch nothing. I know now how this works. So, now I just need to find the correct hiero-glyphic. Ah, here it is!'

He snatched at one of the keys, and pulled. At first nothing happened. 'It is old and stiff,' he said. 'But I can do it.' He pulled again, and something above them began to rumble and groan. It seemed as if the whole ceiling spun around. Nadine realised that was exactly what was happening.

The stones on the ceiling were in concentric circles and some feat of engineering turned each circle independently of the others. As the circles on the ceiling turned, so too did the stones beneath Nadine and the German, and for the first time she noticed that even beneath her were two separate circles of stones. The pathways moved in separate directions, leaving only a narrow ledge on which to stand. The rotation brought her and the German closer together, so she began to run in the other direction, as did he. She imagined it looked a bit ridiculous, but her heart told her she was in grave danger.

She looked for the entrance through which she had come, but it had disappeared. There was no way out.

'Stop!' he cried, raising his pistol as the ground creaked and groaned beneath him. 'Stop, or I will shoot you. You must save me, you must.' His voice was desperate.

'I'll help you, but put the gun away.

There's no need to shoot me.' She began running back to him as he clung to the guard rail, but the ground began to spin faster, and the stones she stood on moved further away from him. Nadine tried hard to run against the turning tide, but the stones spun even faster, so she turned the other way, certain that eventually she would be opposite the young man.

Before she could reach him, the guard rail next to him slid back without warning, and he fell into the abyss with a sickening scream. As he did, the walkway stopped with a judder, throwing Nadine to the ground, and the guard rail miraculously slotted back into place.

Nadine put her head into her hands, a wave of pity washing over her. He had only been a kid; possibly even younger than her. He had believed in his Fuhrer and wanted to please him in much the same way she was trying to please her dead father. Except her father had not been interested in taking over the world. As far as she knew . . .

The stakes were even higher than she had thought and in more ways than one. If she picked the wrong key, she too would plunge into the abyss.

'And I thought archaeology was just digging up old bones,' she said out loud, trying to lighten her mood. 'Except it will be *my* bones they're digging up.'

She took a deep breath and walked the circumference of the circle. The German had gone for the key with a scroll on it. That was clearly too obvious for the engineer who built the chamber. 'Eenie, meenie . . . ' Nadine muttered to herself, pointing up to the keys. 'Be serious,' she chided herself. 'Prudence. Foresight . . . '

She cleared her mind of the clutter and the memory of the recently dead German. If she dwelled on that she was bound to make a mistake.

The two keys would have to bear the same image, but only one of them would be correct. Except the German had tried that and failed. Nadine moved into the light and wondered again where the light source was coming from. It must be reflected from something. 'Reflected,' she muttered. 'Reflected.'

What had the other symbols of prudence been? Book, scroll and mirror. Sometimes the mirror had a snake entwined around it. It took her a while, but she found it. She had expected a hieroglyphic depicting a mirror, but it turned out to be even more obvious than that. As she moved into the light and looked upwards, she saw her own reflection looking back at her from the smooth surface of the bow of one of the keys, whilst a tiny snake wound around its shoulder.

'Oh please, let it be it,' she prayed as she reached up. She pulled, and the key came nearer to her, dragging another key from the centre. It was the literal mirror image of the one she held, right down to the cuts slanting in the other direction.

'Got it!' she cried, as she finally held it in her hand, and unclipped it from the chain. She only just had time to put it away safely when the guardrail and walkway gave way.

'Oh, for goodness' sake!' The words became an echo as blackness engulfed her again.

★ ★ ★

'Is she still alive?'

'Yes, thank God.'

Nadine opened her eyes to see Lance and everyone else surrounding her. She was aware of her clothes sticking to her in wet clumps.

'What . . . ' She tried to sit up. Someone had pulled her out of the water and set her down on the grassy bank.

'Stay still a moment,' Lance commanded. 'You've had a nasty accident.'

'It wasn't . . . ' she began to say, and then thought better of it. She did not want to have to explain her adventures.

'I mean, I must have slipped on the riverbank.'

'And scratched your legs and arms in the process,' Lance said wryly. She got the distinct impression that he did not believe her.

'You are bleeding,' said Prince Ari.

'Gave us a bit of a fright,' Mr Hardcastle cut in.

'My boots,' Nadine said, looking at her bare feet. 'Where are they?'

'Don't worry, they're here,' said Valerie Bentley, bringing the boots forward. 'They're how we found you. They were floating along the riverside, and we recognised them as yours. By the time we found you, an old Arab was pulling you from the water. I think he was the same one from the train, but I couldn't swear to it.'

Nadine looked at everyone standing around her; Lance, the Prince, Mr Hardcastle, Mr Devon, Valerie and the Suttons. Had one of them sent the German after her? Or was it something to do with the old Arab man who seemed to be dogging her movements?

'Where is the old man?' Nadine asked. 'I'd like to thank him.'

'He went away when he saw us,' the prince said. 'Mr Smith carried you to a more comfortable position.

'We'll get you back to the hotel,' Lance said. 'There'll be a doctor there who can look at your head. You might have swallowed some Nile water too. You're gonna feel mighty sick soon.'

'Thank you.' Nadine felt too weak to argue, and she longed to be somewhere private.

The trip back to Cairo seemed interminable. Nadine sat at the edge of the boat clutching her boots the whole way. She eschewed offers of food or drink. She could taste the Nile in her throat, and whether imagined or not, it made her feel queasy. It was a magnificent river, but, like most water-ways that saw heavy traffic, not particularly clean.

At least she was alive. Despite him drawing a gun on her, she half-hoped that the German had survived, but something told her he had not, and that his journey had ended painfully at the bottom of the abyss. She shuddered, and felt Lance put a protective arm around her.

'I'm alright,' she said.

'You're freezing cold, despite the heat. You could be coming down with a fever.'

'No, I'm not. It's just . . . ' Nadine stopped. She wished she could trust Lance enough to share the experience with him, but her father had talked about a German spy with archaeological abilities. What if that man was Lance? She doubted it was the young man who had followed her. He did not seem experienced enough. He was what one might call cannon fodder. It made Nadine feel sadder than she should have about the boy's death, considering he would have been happy to shoot her.

When they got back to the hotel, the countess was waiting for her in the foyer. 'Really, Nadine, you were supposed to be working this morning. What do I find when I return? You've gone out. And goodness knows where. Look at the state of you, girl. What have you been up to?'

'I'm sorry, Countess . . . '

'It is my fault,' the prince cut in, earning a scowl from Lance. 'Miss Middleton only went to post a letter, but I talked her into joining me on an excursion to Elephantine, where sadly she had an accident.'

'Oh, well, why didn't you say so, Your Highness?' The countess's eyes gleamed with satisfaction. 'If you want to spend time with Nadine, then who am I to get in the way of true love? Poor dear.' She turned to Nadine. 'I hope the prince was able to save you.'

'Well, er . . . ' Nadine stammered. The prince caught her eye and winked almost imperceptibly. 'Yes. Yes he did.' For some reason, she did not want to explain about the old Arab. Lance looked even more miserable. He scowled at the prince, who simply smiled back in his normal charming way.

The countess clapped her hands together, happy to believe a lie that fit into her grand romantic scheme. 'My plan is clearly coming together. Nadine, go and rest and I will send a doctor to you. Now, now, Your Highness, I know you cannot bear to be parted from her, but I promise you may sit with us at dinner when we embark on the Nile steamer later this evening.'

'Thank you. I will be honoured.' The prince gave a courteous bow.

When she reached the sanctuary of her room, Nadine hardly had time to check the key was still in place before there was a knock at the door. It was the Egyptian doctor, a serene and gentle man in his fifties. He gave Nadine a thorough check before pronouncing her fit.

'Luckily the damage to your skull is not serious. As for drinking the Nile, I will give you something to help if you start to feel sick. It is important you drink plenty of other fluids, to help flush any germs through your system.'

'Doctor?'

'Yes?'

'You're local.'

'Ah, so you noticed,' he said with a warm smile.

Nadine blushed. 'Do you know about the Eye of the Storm? It's a jewel that is supposed to help one see the future.'

'I have heard such legends, but that is all they are, child. It is not for us to see what lies ahead. Only Allah knows the future. To mess with such things . . . ' He shook his head gravely. 'It is not good. Only darkness will follow.'

'I think the darkness is already here,' Nadine said absent-mindedly. Someone wanted the jewel really badly, and was willing to kill for it. She realised she was being naïve in trusting the doctor, but she reasoned that he could not be connected to any of it.

'You mean with the Nazis? Hmm, they look to our country with hungry eyes, and our king . . . ' The doctor clamped his lips shut. 'These things are not for us to talk about, Miss Middleton. Let the politicians fight it out amongst themselves.'

'Yes, you're probably right.'

When the doctor had gone, she locked her bedroom door and shut the curtains, afraid someone might be spying on her. Then she picked up one of her boots and turned it over, exposing the sole. She pressed the bottom of the shoe and the heel clicked open, revealing the key just where she had hidden it, along with the scrap of paper bearing a copy of the riddle. Luckily her assailant had not thought to look there. Or if they had — because she had not been wearing her boots when she was found — they had been disturbed before they could find the key.

Who had sent the boy? And who was the old Arab who kept turning up? Was he the German spy? Or just someone working for the Germans? All the questions made Nadine's head ache. She lay on her bed and slept for a while, waking up feeling refreshed.

Soon it was time to go to the steamer and begin their trip up the Nile.

Despite Nadine's ordeal, the countess made it clear she expected her to continue her duties. Much of her time was taken up with ensuring the countess's luggage was where it should be, with every trunk and suitcase accounted for — along with a dozen other chores, and that was before she could even begin to sort out her own luggage. She had to remind herself that this was what she had signed on for — at least, as far as the countess was concerned.

Her own cabin was rather small, but she had not expected any different. She did not plan to be in it very often. As much as she could, she intended to take in the scenery.

The shout came up at dusk that they were leaving, and all passengers were encouraged to move to the deck and wave everyone off as the steamer began its journey. Nadine found herself waving at people she did not even know, which made her rather sad and lonely. Her head ached a little and no matter how much mineral water she drank, she could not get rid of the dry feeling in her mouth.

Then, as she scanned the crowds on the bank, she had a strange feeling of familiarity. Someone who she knew was in the crowd, she was sure of it. When she tried to find who or what left her with that sensation, there was no one to be seen. She put it down to wishful thinking, which only made her feel more isolated.

She almost jumped out of her skin when someone put their hand on her shoulder.

'Are you okay?' Lance asked. 'You look spooked.'

'Yes. Yes, I'm fine, thank you. I just thought I saw ... It was nothing, really.'

'Be careful, Nadine,' Lance said.

'We're not in London now.'

'You don't say?' She turned her head, her eyebrow raised.

'No. Soon we'll be a long way from anywhere, and the only escape will be the desert or the river. Neither of which are much good if you don't have proper transport.'

'Are you warning me?'

'I'd have thought that was obvious.'

'No, I mean, are you warning me off?'

'I'm just trying to look out for you. I owe it to your father.'

'You owe my father a lot of things.'

'Yes, I know, and I intend to make it up.'

'You owe me nothing, Lance.'

'If I can take care of you in Raleigh's place, then I will. Or would you prefer the handsome prince to do that?'

'As far as I know, he's never betrayed my father.'

She heard his sharp intake of breath before he moved away, his eyes darkening with some unknown emotion.

The steamer sailed away from the shore, and gradually the twinkling lights of the city were far behind them and they were moving into less populated areas.

Despite the lateness of the day, farmers worked on the riverbanks, using their hands and old-fashioned methods. Occasionally that spell was broken by the sight of a bright new tractor or truck, reminding her that Egypt was a modern country and not some primitive backwater.

Yet she still had an odd sense of drifting back in time. She would not have been surprised to see Cleopatra and Mark Anthony sailing past in a royal barge, oblivious to everything but their love for each other. What might it be like to have the selfish type of love that brought down a kingdom; to feed off each other's vanity and ambition so that the rest of the world and its needs did not matter? Would it be heaven? Or would it be hell? Perhaps it would be a mixture of both.

It was Nadine's belief that love should be unselfish, and that it should make you kinder to others, not crueller. She had never been deeply enough in love to have to put the theory to the test. She was sensible enough to consign her feelings for Lance to her teenage years, and whilst his rejection had stung, she had not been mortally wounded.

That did not explain why his presence unnerved her so much, but she put it down to her distrust of him and the fact that he was probably after the same thing she was. What might he do to get it?

'Nadine!' The countess's shrill voice rang out as darkness descended. 'Nadine, it's time for dinner. Where are you, child? Not fallen in the Nile again, I hope!'

After dinner, everyone met in the salon for a drink. The count and countess, with the prince and Valerie Bentley, played bridge, whilst Nadine sat on one of the long, low sofas next to the window and tried to watch the boat's passage as the night grew darker. Soon, the only lights were those from the boat and they did not stretch far enough to see the bank.

On the other side of the salon, Mr Hardcastle was talking in a loud voice to his secretary, Mr Devon. Devon was about twenty-six, with blond hair, high cheekbones and pale blue eyes. Nadine had yet to see him smile, but she figured that working for Mr Hardcastle was probably not the happiest of roles.

'Make sure you speak to the minister before you go to bed.'

'It is very late, Mr Hardcastle,' said Mr Devon.

'The minister won't mind if it's from me. Get in touch with the Duke of Windsor too ... And organise a birthday present for young Princess Margaret.'

Nadine soon realised that Mr Hardcastle's commands were not for Mr Devon's benefit. Such instructions could have been given in his cabin, before dinner. They were for the benefit of the rest of the passengers. The demands said: 'Look at how important I am, on personal terms with ministers and royalty.'

'Is it true,' asked Miss Sutton, who was sitting at a nearby table with her brother, 'that the duke is a supporter of Herr Hitler?'

Mr Hardcastle opened and closed his mouth, and then appeared to look to Mr Devon for an answer. For a moment, it seemed that their roles were reversed, and that it was Mr Devon in charge whilst Hardcastle awaited orders.

'How should I know?' said Mr Hardcastle, when Mr Devon didn't answer. 'The duke doesn't confide in me.'

'It is said that he not only visited Herr Hitler's retreat in Obersaltzberg but he also gave a Nazi salute,' Miss Sutton carried on. She turned to Nadine. Valerie was busy playing bridge leaving Nadine as the only other female she could include in the conversation. 'I read it in a magazine.'

'That's true,' said Lance. He had been sitting a few feet away from Nadine, very much apart from the rest of the group. Whereas everyone else was dressed in formal evening attire, Lance still wore his usual khaki trousers and leather jacket. As an American, he seemed to be able to get away with informality with no-one raising an eyebrow.

'It's a good job he stood down as king,' said Mr Sutton, in one of his rare contributions to the discussion, 'or he'd have just handed England over to Hitler by now.'

'You don't know that!' Hardcastle protested.

'We really shouldn't be impugning someone's reputation,' Nadine said.

'I think the Duke of Windsor is quite capable of that without my help,' Lance snapped. He stood up and left the room.

'Idiot,' Nadine muttered to herself.

Why could she not just have left things alone? And why did she feel bad about stating the truth about Lance?

The conversation turned then to the impending war, on which everyone had an opinion.

'Just what we need to shake these young 'uns up,' Hardcastle opined. 'It gives a man backbone to fight a war.'

'I don't know how we can tell when so many lost their lives in the last war,' the count said in his mild way.

'I was in the trenches,' Hardcastle bragged. 'Didn't do me any harm. Made me what I am today.'

'A pompous bore?' Miss Sutton murmured to Nadine, who covered her mouth to hide the smile.

'Whatever you think of him, Hitler's got the right idea,' Hardcastle continued. 'Get them into training camps when they're young. Bit of national service would do them all good. Youth nowadays don't respect their elders.'

'Does that respect include the Jews?' the count asked. 'Or the Czechs or the

Poles? Or is it only given to those who agree to Hitler's idea of Aryan perfection?'

'Got nothing against the Jews,' Hardcastle said. 'I've worked with a few over the years.'

'But . . . ' Nadine said, bristling. Her mother had been Jewish.

'But Hitler thinks — and I don't say that he's right — that they had a stranglehold on the German economy. Took the jobs of hardworking Germans. So he says.'

'Most of the Jews in Germany *are* hardworking Germans,' the count said.

'You know what I mean,' Hardcastle said, his face becoming redder than ever. 'You're just twisting my words now. And they're not my words, anyway. They're Hitler's. Like I said, I don't say I agree with him.'

'The problem, Mr Hardcastle, is that if anyone begins a sentence with 'I've nothing against a particular race, but . . . ', then it's clear that nothing good can possibly follow.'

'Now, now,' Hardcastle blustered. 'There's no need to be rude, Count. I've done nothing to you. Ah, I see it now. You're of Jewish extraction, aren't you?'

'I will not answer that, on the grounds that it is not important if I am or I am not,' the count said, lightly.

'I think I'll turn in if there's nothing else you need, Countess,' Nadine said. The air had become brittle with some unknown emotion.

'What?' The countess was deeply engrossed in her cards and had taken very little interest in the discussion. The count, on the other hand, was alert and deeply interested in what was going on around him. He and Nadine exchanged meaningful glances. Yes, she thought, we both feel the same; as if our entire lineage has been impugned. 'Yes.' The countess waved her hand dismissively. 'Yes, go to bed, Nadine. I am not tired yet. My maid will see to anything I need.'

Nadine stepped out of the salon on

the opposite side from her cabin, because she needed some fresh air. She walked partway around the steamer, before bumping into a figure in the shadows.

'Lance! You made me jump.'

He said nothing. He simply looked down at her. She became lost in a spell from which she could not escape. The air was charged with something different now; still undefinable, but not as unpleasant as in the salon.

His arms stole around her waist and he pulled her to him, kissing her passionately. When he let her go, she swayed a little, unsure whether to kiss him back or slap his face for his impertinence. She had to admit that she had needed that kiss after the uncomfortable discussion in the salon. She wanted another, and almost returned the favour, but his hands caught hers as they were about to caress his neck and pull him back to her.

'I had to get that out of my system,'

he said, brusquely. His deep voice trembled a little. He let her go abruptly, and disappeared back into the shadows.

5

After several stops at minor places of interest over a couple of days' travel, the steamer brought them all to Giza. Most of the passengers left the boat for an excursion to the Giza Plateau, where the most magnificent pyramids in Egypt stood.

As Nadine had noticed before, there was an interesting juxtaposition of the old and the new. They travelled, by taxi, through a bustling city with a complete infrastructure, then out into the desert, which was literally on the doorstep of the city.

'This city was built mainly by the British,' the countess told them all, proudly. Nadine wondered what the Egyptian guides would have to say about that, but they were all very polite and obviously used to people like Countess Chlomsky.

'Strange,' said Valerie Bentley, when they reached the plateau. 'One expects the pyramids to be in the middle of the desert, yet here they are, right on the edge of the town.'

'I imagine the undertakers did not want to carry the pharaohs that far,' the count said, with the usual twinkle in his eyes. Then, more seriously, 'What is the use of a monument if no one can see it? The pharaohs wanted to be remembered long after they were gone.'

Everything was arranged to perfection. When they reached the plateau, the tour guides set up tents under which they served a picnic lunch. It allowed the tourists to come and go as they pleased, wandering around the pyramids, before returning for refreshment.

As if by design, Nadine found herself walking with Prince Ari. She could not help wondering if the countess had arranged it. The count and countess had stayed behind at the tent, preferring to admire the pyramids from afar.

'Our old legs cannot cope nowadays,' said the countess. 'But you go, Nadine.'

For Nadine's part, she could only think of Lance's kiss. That had been several days before, and since then he appeared to be avoiding her, keeping to his cabin except at mealtimes.

When she walked with the prince, Lance followed a few yards behind, his hands in his pockets and his head down to the ground. She had thought he would be fascinated by the pyramids, but it occurred to her that he had probably seen them plenty of times.

When Nadine had been alone on the boat, she had time to pore over her father's journal. She had made copies of all the main clues so that she could keep the notebook hidden. But for today, she could relax as there was nothing in Giza that she had to find. She supposed it was because most of the pyramids had been excavated, so it was unlikely anything more could be hidden in them. She could just be a tourist, the same as everyone else. She had to admit that the prince was good company.

'They say it took twenty years to build the Great Pyramid,' he explained, when they reached that structure. 'Can you imagine the effort in dragging those stones across the land to this place? Eight hundred tonnes a day?'

'A lot of people must have died,' Nadine said. In her mind's eye, she could see exhausted slaves, being driven by the whip of a brutal overseer. Despite that, she could only marvel at the structures in front of her.

'Yes, indeed. All so that one day, a group of over-privileged tourists could take tea at its base.'

'I'm sure there was more reason than that,' said Nadine, feeling unaccountably protective of all that history. 'The pharaohs believed they would become gods in the afterlife, didn't they? Whatever we may think of the story behind the building, one has to admire their belief. That same belief, in Britain, led to people dragging heavy stones all the way to Stonehenge. Belief has resulted in some of the most beautiful churches and artwork. We may not approve of the methods, but we can admire the results. And, from a distance, that prevents us from feeling personally responsible,' she added, her cheeks dimpling.

'This is true. I still hate that so many people died so that a king might feel he is immortal.'

'Do you think that the pharaohs might simply have done what was expected of them?' asked Nadine. 'To prove their importance? In the same way that leaders go to war nowadays — to show the people how great they are.'

'Perhaps. But it seems wrong to me that we should always do what is expected of us. Duty is as much a bind as the worst chains upon a slave.'

The prince spoke with some bitterness. Nadine suspected that they had moved from the general to the personal.

'You're unhappy,' she suggested.

'I know I have no reason to be, Miss Middleton. I am wealthy, and I am told that I am not too bad to look at.' He smiled disingenuously. 'Yet I am expected to give up all my own desires so that I may do my duty to . . . my country.'

'You're not Egyptian?'

'My family are from a small country near Nubia. I travel there to take a vow that will keep me in chains for many years to come.'

'Ah. The countess will be very disappointed,' Nadine grinned. 'I am afraid she has already picked out her hat for our wedding.'

The prince smiled, but there was something in his eyes that suggested to Nadine she had misunderstood him somehow. 'You are very lovely, Miss Middleton.'

'But?'

'My heart lies elsewhere.'

'I see.'

'I have offended you?'

'No, Your Royal Highness, not at all. I am grateful for your honesty. And

110

actually quite relieved. You are very handsome and charming.'

'But?' He grinned again, repeating her word back at her. 'I think, perhaps, that your heart also lies elsewhere. There is a history between yourself and Mr Smith, is there not?'

'Oh. No. I mean — yes.' Nadine looked behind to make sure Lance was not too close. He had fallen back somewhat, and was walking with the Suttons. 'I had a crush on him when I was a teenager.'

'A 'crush'?' The colloquialism seemed to confuse the prince.

'It's what we call being in love when it's not really love. The blight of teenage girls all over the planet, I'm afraid.'

'And now, this 'crush' is . . . crushed?' He smiled, and it occurred to Nadine that a girl could get used to that expression.

Nadine looked over her shoulder again. 'He betrayed my father in the worst way. Dad had been Lance's mentor at the university. He not only taught him everything he knew, but he welcomed him into our family. At the same time, Dad was becoming increasingly interested in what one might call 'fringe' science — that is, interest in the more supernatural elements of artefacts. He almost found the Ark of the Covenant once, but someone beat him to it. When Dad went missing, Lance wrote an article for a respected science journal, denouncing Dad as a charlatan and snake oil salesman. He did it only to distance himself from Dad, because his name had become linked with my father's, and he did not want people to think he believed the same . . . as he called it . . . nonsense.' She looked at the prince. 'So, yes, my crush was crushed.'

'It is strange,' said the prince. 'I have spoken to Mr Smith several times, and each time I was sure he was a man who has an open mind. We talked of the Eye of the Storm.'

'Really? What did he say?'

'Only that he thinks it is an artefact of great interest.'

'Perhaps that's why he turned on Dad. Because he wanted to find it himself.' Her hand went instinctively to the back of her head where the lump was starting to heal. Would Lance do such a thing to her? He had often been dismissed as a cowboy archaeologist, and his adventures were the stuff of legend in the English newspapers. But he had always insisted that all artefacts belonged in a museum. He sought no personal advantage from finding them. Unless that was a front. Perhaps, when it came down to it, he was nothing more than a grave-robber and attacker of young women.

They moved on from the pyramids to the Sphinx, a limestone monument of the mythical creature with a lion's body and a human head. It reminded Nadine of the joke about her father and the nose being knocked off, but she chose not to share that with the prince.

As the prince walked around the statue, she sat down to rest. Lance and Valerie Bentley walked past, and both nodded to her, but neither spoke. They seemed to be getting on very well.

Nadine shut her eyes to give them some respite from the blazing sun, or at least from Lance enjoying the company of a very pretty young woman. When she opened them again, she looked across into the desert, and was sure she saw a dark mass of movement. 'Is that a sandstorm?' she asked, but when she looked around there was no one to hear her question. The prince had moved away, and she wondered if she had in fact dozed off for a while.

She stood up and walked towards the desert, careful not to go too far. Soon the mass came closer, and she realised it was made up of about a dozen men on horseback. 'Bedouins,' she murmured. She had never seen them, so it was interesting to her to chart their movement. She knew of their peripatetic lives, moving from place to place. In England, they would be reviled and called gypsies. In the North African desert, they were older than civilisation and regarded with great respect. They had a hierarchy of loyalty that started with the brother and reached out to extended family and the whole community.

She guessed that they were coming into the city for supplies. As they drew nearer still, she waved at them in a friendly manner. Their movements became more purposeful. Within a few seconds, they were surrounding her, and she began to feel worried. She spun around, looking for someone else. For a moment, she thought she saw a figure coming from behind the Sphinx, but the sun was in her eyes so she could not see who it was. She waved frantically, but with the horses surrounding her, she did not think the other person could see her.

Before Nadine could argue or protest, one of the men swooped down and caught her around the waist, lifting her up onto the horse. The whole group rode away into the desert, taking her with them.

6

It was over an hour before they arrived at an oasis somewhere in the middle of the desert. During that time no one spoke to Nadine. The men only rode with grim determination. At first, she fought against her kidnapper, wriggling and attempting to set herself free from his clutches, but found that in the heat of the midday sun, it only made her more exhausted. She knew she would have to preserve her energy for her escape.

When they reached the oasis, she was lifted down from the horse. Her first instinct was to run, but she ran straight into the arms of another one of the men.

'No, no,' he said in broken English. He pulled the mask down from around his lower face, to show a middle-aged man. 'You. Stay. Here.' He smiled at

116

her, and she had the dreadful feeling that he thought he was being friendly.

'I'm not supposed to be here,' she said.

'Yes, yes. My cousin.' He smiled again.

They took her to a tent, where there were clothes laid out. The man who appeared to be the leader said, 'My cousin.' He pointed at the silk garments. 'For you.'

'Cousin? You've brought me here for your cousin? Tell your cousin he can go and — ' Nadine employed words she had only ever heard sailors use. The man looked at her blankly. 'Stay,' he said. 'Wait.'

They left her alone in the tent. Nadine went to the entrance and raised the flap. All around was desert. She had no idea what direction they had come from. For all she knew, there was a city over the next sand dune, just as the pyramids were right on the edge of Giza. But she would not know unless she tried, and she risked walking around in circles until she died of thirst or sunstroke.

She went back in and sat down, folding her legs and her arms resolutely. Whatever the man's cousin wanted, he would not get it from her! Nadine had read a few books about English women being dragged off into the desert, not to mention seeing the films with Rudolph Valentino, and she had never seen the attraction in a man deciding what a woman wanted before she even knew it herself.

After a few minutes, the tent flap lifted and a young woman came in. She was wearing a burkha, with only her beautiful almond-shaped eyes on show. She carried a plate of melon and a jug of water. 'Eat,' she said, putting them down in front of Nadine. 'Drink.'

'Are they keeping you prisoner too?' asked Nadine. 'I could help you to escape. Or you could help me. You probably know the desert better than I do.'

She was not sure, but she had the

feeling that the girl smiled under her veil. 'My cousin.'

'Tell your cousin to go and ... ' Nadine stopped, figuring the poor girl was as much a victim as she was. 'I am Nadine,' she said, pointing to herself. 'You are?' She pointed to the girl.

'Akilah.'

'Hello, Akilah. I hope we can be friends. We can help each other.' Poor kid, thought Nadine. She probably didn't even know she was oppressed.

'Eat. Drink. My cousin,' Akilah said, her eyes shining with a soft smile.

'We don't have to do this,' Nadine said, feeling hot and bothered. Sweat poured from her brow, and it was not just the heat, but the enormity of the situation she found herself in. 'You don't have to do this. Please help me to escape.' Nadine made a gesture like riding a horse. 'Escape?'

Akilah nodded and made the same gesture.

Nadine breathed a sigh of relief. The girl would help her.

'Eat. Drink. My cousin.'

Nadine sighed. They seemed to have gone backwards. She picked up a piece of melon and ate it. She had to admit it did wonders for her thirst. Reasoning she would need the energy, she ended up eating everything on the plate, and drinking all the water.

When she had finished, Akilah took the plate and jug away. She stopped at the entrance to the tent and looked back. 'You. Pretty.'

'So are you,' said Nadine. 'At least, I think you probably are. I can't see your face.'

Hours seemed to pass. She stood at the entrance to the tent, watching the Bedouins go about their business. The men sat in circles, cross-legged and smoking from a hookah. The women either washed clothes with water from the pond, beating them against the rocks, or they baked flat bread. A lamb turned on a spit over an open fire. The smell made Nadine's mouth water. No one bothered her. In fact, they all seemed a little shy in her presence. She put it down to their guilt at kidnapping her, but she could not fight the feeling that something was wrong about the whole set-up. It was true that no-one had harmed her, but maybe they all feared the cousin who had commanded she be brought here.

Late in the evening, Akilah returned with more food. This time she brought tender lamb pieces, pitta bread, cool yoghurt and sweet pastries to follow. Nadine took a bite without really feeling hunger, until the first mouthful, after which her appetite returned and she ate everything with great enjoyment.

Whatever else her captors wanted, they at least treated her well. The men did not bother her at all, and any women passing by the tent only looked in and smiled with their eyes.

She tried again to entice Akilah to steal some horses, but the girl did not seem to understand, only nodding and smiling and repeating the gesture. 'Soon,' she said. Nadine was not convinced they were even on the same wavelength.

She must have dozed off, falling back onto the pile of cushions they had placed for her. She was awoken by a shout and the furore that followed. She jumped up, unsteadily, and went to the entrance, pulling up the flap to look out. It was dark. There were some lanterns attached to each tent, but the night was so dark as to render them almost useless.

There was a group of men on the edge of the camp, talking in irate tones. She tried to pick up the words, but everything was in Arabic.

She left the tent and walked over to see what was going on. There were some horses corralled at the edge of the water. It occurred to her that whilst everyone was busy arguing, she could try to escape. She crept around the edge of the tents, thinking to come up on the horses from behind. If she could try to remember which direction they had brought her from, she might be able to find Giza again.

Suddenly a cry went up. 'Nadine! Nadine, where are you?'

She spun around to see a figure pulling away from the group of men. 'Nadine, wait up. It's me!'

'Lance . . . ' Her heart leapt. Had he really come for her? 'Oh, Lance.' He was dressed in native garb, and she had to admit that if he carried her off into the desert at that moment, she would not argue. She ran into his arms, letting him envelop her in the folds of his robes. She was safe. 'It was awful . . . They were saving me for their cousin or something.'

Lance turned back to talk to the leader of the men in Arabic. Nadine did not understand, but he seemed angry. The man shook his head and replied in more measured tones.

'What is he saying?' Nadine asked, feeling Lance's body stiffen as the man explained something to him.

'He said that you are here because you want to be. When they said 'My cousin', they were calling you that, because they thought you were going to be related to them.'

'No! That isn't true. Why would I? I don't even know who his cousin is. Lance, there's another girl here. Akilah. We must help her.'

Lance spoke to the man again. 'He says that Akilah is his daughter, and that she's perfectly safe.'

'He's lying. He must be. They're . . . ' Nadine almost said 'savages', but to be honest, they had not behaved like savages at all. Well, apart from the whole kidnapping thing. They had fed her and kept her safe. In fact, they had been very friendly to her.

The man was still speaking in rapid-fire Arabic. 'What is he saying, Lance?'

'His name is Mustafa. He said that they had arranged to meet a young English girl in Giza. She was going to elope with his cousin. They thought it must have been you because you waved at them.'

'I was only being friendly.'

'They never meant to harm or upset you, Nadine. They thought you wanted to be here, and they've had trouble understanding why you were so upset at first. They were waiting for someone who spoke English to come and ask you what the problem was. But they couldn't let you wander into the desert alone, or you'd have died. They've been doing their best to keep you safe.'

'Oh . . . Oh . . . I see. And Akilah really is his daughter?'

Lance asked Mustafa about the girl. 'Yes. She's much loved amongst her people, and a very happy, content girl.'

Nadine wished a sandstorm would come and blow her away. On the other hand, they had just snatched her up without a by-your-leave. They might have checked first! But her good nature overtook her anger. 'Please tell Mustafa I'm sorry for the confusion.'

Lance relayed her apology. Mustafa laughed and nodded. 'Mistake,' he said. 'Big mistake.' He looked from Lance to

Nadine. 'Husband?' he asked Lance.

'No. Oh, no.' Nadine shook her head.

Mustafa smiled, then nodded as if in on some secret. 'Husband,' he said, emphatically.

'We'd better get back to Giza,' said Lance. He spoke to the Arab again, and Nadine guessed he was repeating his words.

Mustafa pointed to the distance. He waved his hands wide, and spoke a few words before saying, 'Woosh,' and making a gesture of covering his head with his hand.

'He says there's a sandstorm on the way,' Lance explained. 'It will make travelling back impossible. We'll have to stay here for the night.'

'We can't! People will worry. The countess will worry.' Now that Nadine knew she was not a prisoner, she was eager to be going, if only to prove to herself that she could leave if she wanted to. She felt trapped in the desert and wanted to be back in civilisation.

'She'll worry all the more if you get

buried in a sandstorm. We'll travel across country tomorrow and meet the boat at Abu-Simbel.'

They had no choice but to wait it out. Nadine could not refuse when Lance went into her tent with her. After all, she reasoned, it was only like camping. Besides, his presence would keep others away. She still could not quite believe that it was all a big mistake. On the other hand, the Bedouins could have easily killed Lance. He was heavily outnumbered. Yet they had not.

Akilah brought them more food. She was laughing under her veil. She said something to Nadine in Arabic.

'She said thank you for trying to save her,' Lance translated. 'She is very happy with her family, but she thinks it's very funny that you thought she was being held captive. She thinks you're a very nice person to worry about her the way you did.'

'Tell her I think she's a lovely girl,' Nadine said. After Lance had relayed that, Akilah left them alone whilst they ate.

At first Nadine did not know what to say. She felt rather foolish, especially as she had characterised the Arabs as the sort of people who would snatch an innocent woman. She had felt all along that something was not quite right; but confusion, and the obvious language barrier, had prevented her from seeing the truth.

'I've seen too many films,' she said out loud.

'Ah, *The Sheik*,' Lance laughed and said wryly, 'Good old Rudy Valentino, depicting innocent Arabs as abductors of innocent females.'

'Thank you for coming for me,' she said at last.

'Anytime.'

'How did you know where to find me?'

'I've been following you since they took you. I stole a man's horse. I guess I ought to take it back ... I've been waiting outside the camp all day, to work out the lie of the land. I saw you watching the women earlier, and that's when I began to wonder if you'd really been kidnapped. But I couldn't do anything that might put you in danger.'

'I wonder who they were supposed to take. It's all very odd.'

'Yeah, it is.'

They did not seem to know what to say to each other after that, so they drank their water and sat listening for the storm.

Outside the tent, there was a faint breeze. Very soon it became stronger, and the sides of the tent started to swell and then fall back into place with an alarming 'thwump'. The wind began to howl around them, and sand beat against the outside of the tent.

'Will the tent stay up?' asked Nadine. She remembered a holiday camping in Wales with her parents, where the wind had ripped the tent from its moorings and taken it off into the air. At the time, as a fearless seven-year-old, she had found it hilarious. It was strange how age and experience made one more frightened, rather than less.

'They know how to build them in the desert,' Lance assured her. 'Don't worry. They're used to these storms.'

The tent swelled again, this time rising a few inches above them. Sand flew in through some gaps at the bottom, before the wind dropped again, and the tent fell back to earth.

'Talk to me,' said Nadine, looking around her, wide-eyed. 'Tell me something.'

'What do you want me to talk about?'

'Anything. No, let's start with why you discredited my father.'

'I thought you wanted me to calm you down, not make you more angry.'

'I want to know why. He loved you as a son, Lance. And I . . . I thought of you as family, too.'

'I did it because Raleigh asked me to do it.'

'What?' She looked at him incredulously. 'That doesn't make sense.'

'If you found out about something

that could give immense power to the enemy, which they could use to chart their assault on the innocent, what would you do?'

'I'd use it for good instead.'

Lance threw back his head and laughed. 'Yes, that's always the paradox. That something used for great evil could also be used for great good. But even the best of men could be swayed by that amount of power, Nadine. They might tell themselves they're doing it for the good of mankind, but who is to decide what's best for the world? In the end, even the most virtuous man — or woman — would become corrupted by that power.'

'You're talking about the Eye of the Storm,' Nadine said. It was a statement rather than a question.

'I am.'

'But you don't believe all that nonsense.'

'Not publicly, I don't. But privately, working alongside your father, I've seen things that defy logic. The truth is that certain people became interested in the Eye of the Storm, and the only way to stop them from being interested was to dismiss it all as superstitious nonsense.'

'And Dad asked you to do that?'

'Yes.'

Nadine shook her head. 'I'm not sure I believe you. He died, Lance. If he's dead, no-one can follow him anywhere, so what does it matter if the Eye of the Storm is true or not?'

'Oh, I don't know.' Lance raised an eyebrow. 'Say he couldn't bear to get rid of his research. Call it vanity. Call it sentimentality. Then say he sent it to someone he knew he could trust. Someone who was above reproach.'

'So?' Nadine asked, pointedly. 'Did he send it to you?' She knew the answer, but she was not yet ready to trust him.

Lance laughed. 'No, he didn't trust me enough to let me have it. I'm too much like him. I'll follow the clues wherever they lead, regardless of the consequences. Can you understand that thirst for knowledge? That need to know, even if knowing destroys you? Your father recognised it in me, which was why he guided me. He said he always wished . . . ' Lance stopped speaking. 'Well, never mind that.'

'He wished he'd had a son,' Nadine finished for him. Her heart hung heavy in her chest.

'He loved you. Don't ever doubt that. He said you were the one good thing he did in his life. That's why he trusted you with his journal.'

'What makes you think I have it?'

'The package that followed you all over Europe and the Middle East? The fact that you went to the Nilometer, which I know is the site of one of the Keys of Virtue.'

'Did you knock me out?' Nadine sat back on her heels, instantly put on her guard.

'I would never hurt you. Why do you think I rode across the desert?'

'Because you want the journal.'

'Unless you have it on you, it would

be a bit pointless. I'm guessing you've hidden it well.'

'Because you're trying to pretend that I can trust you.'

'Jesus . . . ' Lance shook his head. 'I promised your dad that I'd take care of you. Whether you want it or not, I'm going to keep that promise.'

Nadine looked at his face for a long time. He appeared to be speaking in earnest, but she was also struck by his confession that he had an unquenchable thirst for knowledge. She already knew he was ambitious. If he found the Eye of the Storm, what would he do with it? He already had the charm and the looks. Whole careers in politics had been built on much less. Hitler was a good case in point. He was a little toad of a man, yet somehow had the charisma to lead a whole country. What might a spectacular man like Lance do with so much knowledge?

But she felt so alone, and was desperate to trust someone. 'All right. I'll trust you. For now. Dad did send me his journal. I have the first key. What did you call it? A Key of Virtue? It's Prudence. If I'm reading dad's journal correctly, the next one is at Abu Simbel. The journal isn't with me,' she added quickly. 'But I've memorised a lot of it.'

'Your father said you had a good memory.'

'For things written down, yes.' She smiled modestly. 'But I can never remember where I put my gloves.'

He took her hand. 'Good, because they only cover up how lovely your hands are.' She could feel herself being drawn in by his eyes and his rugged good looks. There was a scar on his chin, and she had always wanted to ask him how he got it, but was afraid the answer would be prosaic. She would rather think he had done some daring deed than just slipped in the bathtub. That thought made her blush.

'What are you thinking?'

She did not want to say, 'I'm thinking of you in the bathtub,' so she just shook her head and said nothing.

A howl of wind broke their reverie. The storm rose to an alarming pitch. Another loud 'thwack' of the tent later, and Nadine threw herself into Lance's arms. She half-cursed herself for behaving like a helpless female, and half-enjoyed the feel of his strong embrace. Most of the academics she knew through her father were weedy types, but Lancaster Smith was all muscle. He really was the cowboy archaeologist, toned by years of horse-riding and digging out tombs.

'This storm is terrible,' she said, hiding her head in the crook of his neck.

'Oh, I'm quite enjoying it.' She could feel his body shaking with laughter.

'Oh you!' She beat her fist on his chest playfully. 'If I didn't know better, I'd say you planned this.'

'The storm? Oh yeah, I can call up the elements anytime I want.'

'Tell me about the things you and dad found. The supernatural things.'

'Why?'

'Because it will take my mind off the storm.' *And take my mind off how good it feels to be this close to you*, she thought but did not say.

He looked down at her, his eyes warm and inviting. 'I've kinda forgotten everything I ever learned for now.'

'What happened to that unquenchable thirst for knowledge?'

'I'm thinking I'd like to know other things.'

'What? Are you saying you don't know those . . . other things?'

'I've had my moments.' His lips twisted into a wicked grin.

'I haven't.'

'What?'

'I haven't had my moments,' Nadine confessed. 'Or anyone else's moments, for that matter.'

'It's okay.' He stroked her hair as if she were some revered being. 'We'll just wait out the storm.'

That was what they did. At some point during the night she fell asleep in his arms, only a little disappointed that he had not taken advantage of the situation.

When they awoke the next morning, it was to find half of the camp buried in sand.

7

Before leaving for Abu Simbel, Lance and Nadine felt duty-bound to help the Bedouins dig out the tents that were covered. Thankfully no one was in them, as most of the company had gone to one of the larger tents unaffected by the storm damage.

It meant that it was mid-morning before Nadine and Lance could leave. She was surprised to find that Mustafa and Akilah were going to accompany them.

'They know this desert better than I do,' Lance explained. 'And Akilah is going back to college in Luxor.'

'College?'

'She's training to be a doctor.'

Once again, Nadine's misconceptions were being challenged. First she had mistaken the Bedouins for a savage race — though even they would admit that appearing to kidnap her might give someone that impression. Then she had thought of them as a simple people, living mainly off the land. Now she learned that Akilah was going to have the sort of career she could only dream about.

It made her feel a little bit inadequate. Although she had idly thought of becoming an archaeologist like her father, she had never really had his thirst for knowledge. In fact, she was not sure what she wanted from life. She knew it was not just a home and family, although she wanted those too. Proving her father was dead would unlock a legacy that meant she could do whatever she wanted, but she began to realise that was the easy way out. If she had the money, would she really do anything with her life? Or would she just be one of those women who spent all their time going to charity lunches and holidaying in the south of France? There had to be more that she could do . . .

'You've gone quiet,' Lance said as they rode across the desert.

'I'm thinking that I'm a pretty useless excuse for a human being, really.'

'No, you're not.'

'I am, and nothing you can say will change my mind. If I can find this stone, then maybe I can prove myself to the world.'

'Careful,' said Lance. 'You know the dangers of the stone.'

'Yet you still want to find it.'

'No, I want to keep you safe. Since I know you're going for it anyway, I'm just along for the ride.'

'Hmm,' she said, not entirely sure he was telling the truth. Perhaps that was what people did with the stone. They lied to themselves and others about what they really wanted from it. And was she not doing the same? It was a conundrum, and one she felt she did not have to answer just yet.

They reached Abu Simbel around the same time as the tourists from the steamer. They jumped down off the horses and said their farewells to Mustafa and Akilah.

'Nadine!' The countess's voice rang out across the complex of temples. She was sitting on a stone slab just beneath the feet of one of the colossal statues of the Ramses. The statues, four in all, stood twenty metres high, and depicted the king wearing the double crown of Upper and Lower Egypt. One of the statues had been damaged in an earthquake. In front of him, around the feet of each mighty figure, were statues of his consort, Nefertari, and his children.

'Where have you been? I thought you'd run off with some desert sheik. And look at the state of you, girl. You've gone native. Now go back to the boat and smarten yourself up.'

'I'd like to look around the monuments,' Nadine said.

'Not looking like that, you won't. Don't you realise that you are my ambassador? Your appearance and behaviour reflects upon me.'

If Nadine were honest, she could do with a bath and a change of clothes, but she hated to be bossed around like a recalcitrant schoolgirl. She was also a little put out that no one else seemed to have worried for her safety.

Just as Nadine was turning away, Prince Ari came from within the temple. 'Miss Middleton!' He dashed over to her. 'I am so glad you are safe, dear lady.' He took her hands in his and gave her one of his dazzling smiles. 'I wanted to join Mr Smith in his quest to find you, but he was insistent that only he could save you. You were treated well, I hope? Not harmed?'

'No, my kidnappers turned out to be really rather nice,' Nadine assured him. 'As kidnappers go . . . Not that I've had much experience of being abducted.'

'Happens to me all the time,' Lance said, wryly.

'Good. Good, I am glad,' said the prince, causing Lance to raise an eyebrow in question. The prince smiled and then clarified his words. 'I would

143

not forgive myself if anything had happened to you, Miss Middleton.' He seemed strangely relieved.

'Nadine . . . ' The countess tapped her foot on the floor.

'Yes, Countess.' Nadine started to walk away, but could not resist turning back and saying to her, 'It's so lucky that you assumed I was safe and not being forced into white slavery.' The count, sitting next to his wife, smiled knowingly.

'We knew that Mr Smith had the situation in hand,' he said, as if making excuses for his wife.

'Yes, of course,' said the countess. 'We're British. It does not do to panic in such situations.'

'No, we can't have that, can we?' Nadine walked across to the steamer, which was moored about a hundred yards away from the temple. Yes, Lance had cared, and the prince had shown a modicum of concern; but if not for Lance, no one would have worried about her. It made her feel lonelier than ever.

Not so long ago she had a mother and a father, and whilst her father might not always have been there, she knew she was loved. Who was there to worry about her now? Lance appeared to care, but she was still not sure she trusted him. She conceded that she did need him. He knew more about archaeology than she did, and he spoke the language. But she would have to watch him. She might have spent the night innocently lying in his arms — thinking not-very-innocent thoughts — but she must be careful not to give him her heart.

Back at the boat, Nadine bathed and changed into a pretty dress. She hoped to return to the caves of Abu Simbel, but by the time she had eaten everyone else returned, and the countess made it clear she expected Nadine to resume her duties. The rest of the day was taken with typing up the countess's notes.

The chapters that Nadine worked on

did at least explain why the countess was obsessed with princes. It told the story of the Heart of Cariastan, a precious ruby, which had been given to the countess as a gift by a playboy prince. There followed a workmanlike description of how the jewel became part of a heinous plot, also involving a prince and an ordinary girl. The countess had clearly played up her own part in the proceedings, making out that she had solved the whole thing. Like Miss Marple, but in a tiara, and with wittier repartee as she demolished the bad guys. Nadine had already spent a month in the countess's company, and she had never known her to be that witty.

It was soon time for dinner, so Nadine went to join the others in the dining room. As she walked along the deck, she looked out to the bank and saw Prince Ari talking to an Egyptian. Prince Ari was gesticulating and saying something in Arabic, sounding very angry as he did so. He looked contrite and humble, bowing his head and holding out his hands in supplication. The man turned slightly and Nadine realised that it was Mustafa.

They both appeared to realise that she was watching them, so the two men waved and smiled, then walked away, still talking earnestly, but in lower voices.

Nadine watched them, trying to gain some insight into why the two men were together. Mustafa had not mentioned knowing Prince Ari, and when she related the story of her abduction to everyone at Abu Simbel, the prince had not said he knew Mustafa. What were they involved in together?

She could only assume it had something to do with her father and the journal. Perhaps Prince Ari wanted it and had arranged her abduction. Mustafa must have only let her go with Lance when he realised she did not have it. Yet no one had searched her at the Bedouin camp. They had tried to encourage her to change her clothes. There had been all that stuff about her marrying their cousin, but she decided that must have been a cover story, to explain why she had been kidnapped.

'Penny for them,' said a voice in the dark.

'Lance . . . ' She smiled. Hearing his voice soothed her. 'Prince Ari and Mustafa know each other. I've just seen them arguing together.'

'Sure?'

'Positive.'

'That's strange.' Lance stood at the rail and looked out. The prince and Mustafa had disappeared behind a small sand dune. 'Do you like the prince?' Lance's question was loaded with meaning.

'Yes, I like him. He's very handsome, charming, and attentive. He's not like a prince at all. I thought they were quite grand, but he seems down-to-earth.'

'A simple yes would have done.'

Nadine grinned. Was Lance really jealous? 'Now ask me if I trust him?'

'Do you trust him?'

'I don't trust anyone.'

'How can you like someone but not trust them?'

'Oh,' Nadine sighed. 'Very easily.'

Lance turned to look at her. 'So you don't trust me.'

'I don't trust anyone at the moment. I've just been typing up the countess's autobiography. It's horrifying what people will do for precious jewels. And that's what this is really about, Lance. Not some mystical insight into the future, but a precious jewel. Men have killed for less, and I've already seen one man die because of it.'

'I haven't killed anyone, Nadine. I want to find it for the same reason your father did. To prove him right and to protect others from it.'

'That's the irony, isn't it, Lance? We find it so no one else can. Why don't we just leave it there, so then no-one can have it?'

'They've already found their way to one of the sites. It's a race to find it before our enemies do.'

'They found their way because they

followed me there,' Nadine pointed out. 'If I had any sense, I'd throw my father's journal into the Nile; then no-one could have the information.'

'Why don't you do that?'

'Because it's all I have left of him and the only way I can clear his name.'

'So, we go after the keys, and when we find the jewel, we decide for ourselves what to do with it.'

'What do you know about it, Lance?'

'I know that it's supposed to be a perfect sapphire — about the colour of your eyes.'

'Oh, please.' Nadine sighed.

'I can't say anything to make you trust me, can I?'

'You could avoid treating me like some vacuous debutante.'

Lance opened his mouth to speak, but was halted by the sound of the dinner gong. They went into the restaurant and took their places. Nadine went to sit with the prince and the count and countess whilst Lance sat with the Suttons and Valerie Bentley.

The rest of the evening was taken up with dinner and then more time in the salon, playing bridge. Nadine once again sat on one of the side sofas, watching everyone. It never ceased to amaze her that the British could go anywhere in the world and still behave as if they were in Britain. Even the Egyptian staff catered more for English passengers than any other, ensuring they stocked Scotch and real ale. There was also Earl Grey tea for those who preferred not to drink alcohol.

Valerie came to sit next to her. 'Do you mind?' she asked.

'Not at all.' Nadine smiled. 'It's nice to see you again.'

'You've had quite an adventure.'

'Really?' Nadine raised an eyebrow. 'I'd almost forgotten, everything here seems so normal.'

'We were all very worried,' Valerie assured her. 'I'm sure the countess cared more than she let on. Did your kidnappers happen to mention who they thought they were taking?'

'No. Which is odd. You'd think they'd have wanted to clear up the confusion.'

'Yes, I see what you mean. It's all very intriguing.'

'I'm not sure that's what they really wanted,' Nadine confided.

'Oh?' Valerie looked concerned.

'No. I think they were after something else. I'm lucky they didn't kill me when they realised I wasn't the right person.' Nadine almost told Valerie about the prince talking to Mustafa, but she changed her mind.

Soon it was bedtime. Nadine thought to go back to Abu Simbel during the night, but even she realised that would be a silly thing to do. She would have to find a way back there the next day. Besides, she was worn out from the excitement of the day before. She fell asleep almost immediately.

At some point in the night, she awoke and thought she heard a splash outside her bedroom window, but she put it down to her imagination and went straight back to sleep.

The following morning she joined the count and countess on the deck for breakfast.

'Nadine, something dreadful has happened,' said the countess, before biting into a croissant.

'What is it? Are you ill, Countess?'

The old lady swallowed her food with gusto. 'No, I am well. But early this morning when the steward went to wake Prince Ari, he was gone. Disappeared. No one knows where he is.'

'Has he left the boat?' Nadine asked.

The count shook his head. 'No one could leave without the guard on the gangplank knowing about it.'

'Last night,' said Nadine, 'I thought I heard a splash. Then I thought I'd imagined it.'

'Your room is on the starboard side, is it not?' asked the count.

'Yes, that's correct.'

'There's no guard on that side,' the count informed them, his brow furrowing. 'Few would be foolish enough to try to swim across Lake Nasser, and the prince did not strike me as a foolish man.' He got up and left the women to their breakfast.

Nadine picked at a piece of melon, her appetite gone. What was going on? First the prince talked to Mustafa, and then he disappeared. Was he the cousin that they thought they were taking Nadine for? It put a slightly different slant on the prince's character if he was willing to abduct his women . . . She shook her head. No, that could not be that. He did not seem the type. He had only ever treated Nadine and the other women on the tour with respect and dignity.

A few minutes later, Lance joined them, and heard the story of the disappearing prince. The conversation was repeated several times as the other tourists joined them.

'Probably just gone off on some business,' Hardcastle said. 'Where's my bacon and eggs, Devon? What is this rubbish? Grapefruit? A man cannot live by grapefruit alone.' He laughed at his own joke, but no one else did.

'I saw him talking to someone last night,' Nadine said, but she fell short of saying it was Mustafa. Having already had her misconceptions challenged, she did not want to be caught out again. Yet it seemed odd that the prince had not mentioned knowing Mustafa when the Bedouin had ridden up to the temples with them. They had parted ways quickly, so that Akilah could return to her college; but, even so, the prince must have seen him.

The count did not come back immediately, but about half an hour after he left, they heard a commotion on the starboard side. Then there was a shout and chaos ensued.

Count Chlomsky returned then, slightly breathless. 'It is most tragic,' he said. 'Most tragic indeed. They have just pulled a body from the river, and he has been identified. It appears that the prince has taken his own life.'

8

The tourists spent the day in stunned silence, broken only by the occasional quiet discussion on how wrong it all seemed. The prince had been so handsome and vibrant, and he had not been very old. The thought of him dying was absurd, let alone the idea of him taking his own life.

Because of the tragedy, the steamer was forced to stay moored whilst the authorities came to investigate.

The group moved from the upper deck to the salon then out onto the veranda, switching places on the boat as the mood took them, yet always staying together as a group, as if it afforded them some protection against the bad luck that had befallen the steamer.

Death was a great leveller, thought Nadine. No matter how rich or poor you were, it waited for you. And for some reason, it had caught up with the prince much too soon.

'He always seemed so cheerful,' Miss Sutton said, when they had moved to the railings to watch the comings and goings of the authorities.

Mr Hardcastle agreed. 'Yes, a good man. Devon, go and send that telegram to Winston Churchill like I asked you, there's a good fellow.'

Nadine cringed at Mr Hardcastle's business-as-usual tone, but she understood that none of them really knew the prince. He had been a travelling acquaintance, nothing more. She wondered if she should tell the authorities about the prince's discussion with Mustafa, but something held her back. She had not seen Mustafa on the boat, and the prince had been alive at dinner the night before, so there was nothing to say he had a hand in the prince's death.

'I don't feel like working today,' the countess told Nadine. She suddenly looked very old. 'I think I'll go back to my cabin and rest. So don't do any typing today, child.' Her voice was kinder than usual. 'The tapping would only strain my nerves.'

'Are you ill, Countess?' Nadine asked. 'I could fetch the doctor.'

'No, I am well. It is just . . . well, these things seem to happen around me and I know everyone will expect me to solve the crime.' Her tired old eyes gleamed with quiet pride.

'You think it was a crime?'

'Oh, these things generally are. I really think the criminals of the world want to test me. I will keep out of the way. Meanwhile, I will let you do some snooping around. You can report back to me at dinner tonight.'

'Oh.' Nadine's eyes widened. She was no sleuth herself, but the countess's command did give her an excuse to explore for her own reasons. 'Of course. I wonder . . . well I think the key to this mystery might be at Abu Simbel. May I go there?'

'Yes, good thinking. That was the last

place we really saw him.'

'And at dinner last night,' Nadine reminded her.

'Well, yes of course. But mainly at Abu Simbel.'

'I'll come with you,' Lance said. He had been standing a little apart from everyone, lost in his own thoughts.

Nadine tried to think of a way to stop him, but it would have seemed churlish and rather odd in front of everyone. 'Would you like to come, Valerie?' she asked her friend.

Valerie had also been lost in thought, a dreamy look in her eyes. 'What? Oh, no; I think I'll take a leaf out of the countess's book and rest today.' She yawned and smiled winningly. 'Travelling in luxury is surprisingly tiring, isn't it?'

Miss Sutton and her brother shook their heads before Nadine even had a chance to speak. 'We have things to do,' Miss Sutton said. Yet she showed no signs of moving from her place at the rail where she watched the authorities and the workers go about their business.

'I'll change first,' Nadine told Lance. She had been wearing one of her pretty summer dresses, and she wanted something more suitable for delving into historical sites. She donned her khaki shirt and shorts, slinging a satchel over her shoulder into which she had put some tools for digging. She would not be caught out again.

They left the boat and walked across to the temples. There were only a few other tourists near the site, and they mostly sat down in front of the temples or took photographs. The heat meant that no one was doing much walking around.

'What are we looking for?' Lance asked.

'The next cardinal virtue is justice. I imagine it's something to do with that.'

'The motifs of justice are the sword, scales, or the crown,' Lance explained. 'So something along those lines.'

His advice came so quickly, she

wondered how much he actually knew.

They went up to the entrance of the Great Temple, where there was a bas-relief showing the falcon-headed god Ra Harakhti. He held a feather in one hand, and Ma'at, the goddess of truth and justice, in the other.

'Ma'at had a part in the creation of the universe,' Lance told her. 'She brought order from chaos.'

'So it might be something to do with her,' Nadine suggested. 'Or is that too easy?'

'Who knows? The people who built these temples liked their puzzles.'

They entered the Great Temple and immediately became immersed in the many rooms. The temple became narrower as they went deeper into the many chambers. There were so many monuments and friezes that it was impossible to know where to start.

'What else did Ma'at do?' Nadine asked Lance. 'I mean, apart from bringing order from chaos.'

'In the Egyptian underworld, she

weighed the hearts of the dead against a single feather. That's why Egyptian mummies were always buried with their hearts, even when all the other organs were taken away. If their heart was lighter or the same weight as Ma'at's feather, it meant they were pure and could go on to Aaru, which is pretty much the same as the Elysian Fields beloved by Romans. If not, the goddess Ammat devoured the deceased's heart, and the deceased remained in the underworld.'

'Like Christian Purgatory?'

'Yeah, pretty much. Every faith has their own version of the afterlife and their own gatekeepers. For Ma'at, the dead have to utter forty-two negative confessions, such as 'I have not lied', 'I have not committed adultery', and so on. But they're specific to a person. Not like the Christian Ten Commandments that everyone must follow.'

'So, as long as you have forty-two, it doesn't matter what else you've done?'

'You got it.'

They moved deeper into the temple complex. As they did, it became cooler, the heat from the sun failing to penetrate the stone walls.

Eventually they reached the sanctuary, where the Pharaoh or high priest gave offerings to the gods.

'It's a pity it's the wrong time of year,' Lance said. 'On certain days, the sun shines all the way through the temple, lighting up the reliefs.'

'Good job I brought a torch, then,' Nadine said, taking it out of her bag.

Lance smiled. 'You're a regular Girl Guide.'

'I could never remember the oath. So much for my brilliant memory!'

'Maybe you just didn't believe in it.'

'I must admit, I always thought I'd rather be in the Scouts.'

'I bet the Scouts would have agreed with you.'

'I just wish I knew what we were looking for.' She shone the torch around the walls, but nothing jumped out at her as being the right motif. 'In

Dad's journal there was a riddle: '*Rouse the core, to open the floor*'. You read hieroglyphics,' she said to Lance. 'Doesn't anything strike you as being correct?'

'I'm thinking . . . ' Lance walked around the walls, looking up at each image in turn. It was ten minutes before he found anything. 'Here . . . if we take 'core' to mean the heart . . . ' He pointed to some writing on one of the reliefs. 'It says, '*Ma'at, awaken within our hearts. Open the chamber that we may find . . . balance.*' It's not actually 'balance', but that's the nearest word I can find to it.'

'I'm guessing that reading it out loud doesn't do the trick,' Nadine said, joining him. 'Or anyone who reads hieroglyphics can open it.'

'No, you're right. It's never that simple.'

Nadine reached up and ran her hand over the images. When she got to the symbol for 'heart', she pressed a little harder. After all, it had been that easy at the Nilometer. She waited, but nothing happened. The rock under her fingers did not shift, and neither did the floor.

Nadine sighed and wandered to the far wall of the sanctuary. 'It's no good,' she said. 'It's not working ... ' Suddenly the stone beneath her started to move. She looked down — which was the one place they had not thought to look — and saw that there was a pair of scales cut into the rock. 'Lance!'

He dashed across and jumped onto the stone platform in time. They clung together. The stone appeared to hang in mid-air as it lowered deeper and deeper into the cavernous rock. 'It must have been the words,' said Nadine. 'It must have been, because thousands of people have stood on this stone.'

'Maybe,' said Lance, looking at her with renewed interest.

They descended to at least three hundred feet below the temples. When they reached the ground — and yet another cavern that seemed to have a light source coming from nowhere

— they jumped off the stone slab just before it started its ascent back to the top.

'What's holding it?' Nadine asked, looking underneath. She could see nothing connecting the stone to any sort of mechanism.

'Don't ask,' said Lance. 'We may need to get back on it, and if you think about it too much, you won't do it.'

Instead they looked around the cavern. Murky water trickled down the walls, presumably coming from Lake Nasser above them. Whilst the cavern itself seemed to be a natural phenomenon, there were four man-made archways leading off it.

Nadine was relieved to see that there were no black pits this time, but she wondered what other perils awaited them.

'Take your pick,' Lance said, pointing at the arches.

Instead, Nadine walked from one to the other, looking at the inscriptions on the lintels. 'Do any of these match the hieroglyphics we read in the upper chamber?'

Lance followed her and they came to the fourth door, which Nadine guessed was to the east. 'This one.'

'So we follow this one,' she said, taking the lead.

'Yes, ma'am. After you.'

'No, after you. You're supposed to be the big strong man.'

'I know, but I was thinking of equality: women getting the vote, and all that jazz.'

'I'll let you have this one,' she quipped, pushing him under the archway. Strange how free and easy they could be with each other, considering she did not trust him one iota.

They walked for a long way down a narrow corridor, before that opened into another cavern. It was definitely man-made, decorated with monuments of pharaohs and gods. In the centre was a set of stone scales some thirty feet high and twenty feet wide, with a stone plinth between the weighing pans, which were about five feet across. On one of the weighing pans was a pile of feathers.

'I wonder how long the feathers have been there,' Nadine pondered. 'Why haven't they turned to dust?'

'Maybe they're replenished every now and then,' Lance suggested. He pointed to the roof where there was a metal grid. 'Through there. Listen . . . ' They could hear birds cooing and the scratch of claws on the ceiling. Several feathers floated down, and when they landed on the scale, a couple fell off from the bottom.

'It's like one of those penny arcade games,' Nadine said. 'Where you use your pennies to push the others off the edge.'

'So, what do we do? I'm guessing it's nothing to do with pennies.'

There were steps leading up to one side of the scales. 'I suppose someone sits on one of the pans.'

'You're the lightest.'

'But this isn't about physical weight,

Lance,' Nadine reminded him. 'If this is Ma'at's test, this is about spiritual weight. The sins we've committed. Or haven't committed, if your theory about the reverse commandments is true.'

'Like I said, you're lighter.'

'Are you mocking me — ?' She almost added 'because I'm a virgin', but she did not want to admit that to him. Besides, she might need it for her reverse confession, and she did not want to use it up too soon.

'I'm not mocking you, honey. I'm just stating a fact. Go on, up you get.'

Nadine grimaced at him and then started to climb the steps.

She halted next to the scales, unsure whether to risk it. 'This is all a bit silly.'

'We'll see,' said Lance. He stood watching her, and that made her even more nervous.

'If someone comes to eat my heart, I expect you to save me,' she said.

'Whatever happens, I promise your heart is safe with me, darlin'.'

Unsure how to answer that one, she

sat down on the stone scale. It immediately swooped down, causing her to cry out loud. As it lowered, the floor beneath her opened up.

'Oh, *now* it shows me the deep dark pit,' she muttered. 'I thought they'd have some new ideas; but, oh no, just another black hole, leading God knows where.'

'Quickly!' Lance called. 'Remember the reverse confessions.'

'Oh . . . I have not . . . I have not lied,' Nadine said, but the scale only swooped lower. 'All right, I have not lied to intentionally hurt anyone.' The scale did not move upwards, but neither did it fall any further.

'I have not committed adultery.' The scale moved slightly higher.

'I have not coveted my neighbour's . . . lawnmower.' The scale didn't move.

'Try a bit harder. You need forty-two,' Lance reminded her. 'And you must name a god.'

'Forty-two? I can't think of forty-two interesting things I haven't done! And I only know of one God.' The scale started to swing violently. 'Oh . . . I haven't stolen anything from my fellow man. I dedicate that one to, erm . . . Jesus.' The scale moved upwards.

'It doesn't matter if it's an Egyptian god or your own,' Lance said. 'As long as it's the truth of your heart.'

'Okay . . . I haven't killed anyone. That's for . . . oh, Saint Peter. Is he a god?' The scales seemed to think so, and rose a couple of inches.

'It's whatever, or whoever, is in your heart,' Lance said. 'Keep going.'

'I have not stolen the apples of my . . . grocer.' Nadine named another apostle. She carried on in that vein, working her way through Matthew, Mark, Luke and John, and then on to Saint Paul. The scales fell a bit when she mentioned his name, but she had never had much liking for Saint Paul and his opinion of women, so she quickly changed it to Mary Magdalene and the scales rose again.

She was running out of things to say

when the scale on which she sat drew almost level with the scale bearing feathers.

'You need to be higher,' Lance said. 'Just three more to go.'

'I have not dishonoured my father,' Nadine said. 'That's for the Holy Ghost. I think. I have not committed a robbery with violence. Or without violence, for that matter. Is that one or two?'

The scale moved so that it was level with the other scale. 'That should be it,' she said. 'You said it either had to balance or get higher. It's balanced.'

'It was balanced when we started. You need to go higher.'

'Okay . . . ' She had been avoiding saying it, because Lance was there, and it seemed too intimate. But they needed the other key, and she didn't want to fall into the dark pit. 'I have not lain with a man. I'll dedicate that one to God himself.'

The scale swooped almost up to the ceiling. 'Is that it?' said Nadine.

'Nothing has happened ... ' She looked up, and that was when she saw it, cut into a recess. She reached up and grabbed the key, quickly putting it in her pocket, after which she suddenly swooped down again, and the seat on the scales tilted.

Nadine clung to the centre, but the rock was smooth and she could find no purchase.

She thought she would fall into the pit again, but as she fell, strong arms caught her and pulled her onto safe ground.

'Oh, Lance. Thank God.' She clung to him, afraid that if she let go, she would fall again. 'Can you hear something?' It was a dry, rasping sound.

They looked around and saw that small holes had opened up in the walls, through which poured tons of sand . . .

9

'We have to get out before it buries us,' Lance said, somewhat redundantly.

'I gathered that.' When Nadine looked for the entrance through which they came, it had disappeared. They had been so engrossed in the scales that they had not noticed it closing.

Nevertheless, they ran to it, and saw there was a seam around the edge where the doorway had been. They pushed with all their might. When that didn't work, they tried to slide it across. At the same time, the tons of sand were quickly filling the chamber behind them.

'They don't mean anyone to be getting away with these keys,' Nadine said, sweat pouring from her brow. Her finger nails were split and ragged from scratching at the door. 'I don't understand. If I passed the balance test, why can't I have the key?'

'You probably have to pass every test,' Lance explained. He too was sweating from exertion, his soaking wet shirt sticking to his back. Nadine guessed that it made him look much sexier than it did her. 'That includes finding a way out.'

Sand formed around their feet, and was almost up to their ankles. They managed to pull their feet out and get up onto the higher level, but the pouring sand was relentless, and pretty soon their feet were covered again. 'We have to get higher,' Nadine cried. 'Quickly, to the scales.'

They clambered through the sand, and climbed the steps to the scales, jumping onto the balance tray. Immediately the tray swooped down until it was almost level with the sand. Soon the sand would cover it and they would be back to square one. 'Damn!' Nadine groaned. 'Come on, Lance. Your turn. Tell me all your non-sins.'

'I don't have any. I've pretty much

done it all. Except killing, I guess.'

'There must be something good that you did! It just has to be the truth.'

'Okay . . . I didn't dishonour Raleigh Middleton. I didn't betray his trust.'

To Nadine's amazement, the scales began to fly higher.

The scales raised further still, so they were well out of reach of the sand. She could only look at him in wonder. If the scales did detect the truth, then he had been honest.

Still the sand filled the chamber and there was no way out that they could see. 'One more, Lance. We have to believe it will work.'

'I didn't let Nadine down or betray her trust.'

They heard a metallic sound and suddenly the upper chamber was filled with white doves. The grille had opened. It was a couple of feet away from them, and the sand was not quite high enough for them to walk on, so Lance reached across and then jumped, managing to catch the end of the grille before he fell. He clambered up, presumably into some chamber above, and then he reached down for Nadine. 'Jump,' he said.

'I can't . . . ' Nadine had never been very good at gymnastics at school. 'I really wasn't a very good Girl Guide, Lance.'

'Come on, Nadine. It's a leap of faith. Believe that I will catch you.'

She closed her eyes and did as he said. Two seconds later, she hung in the air like a trapeze artist, as Lance's strong hands enclosed hers. Her shoulders felt as if they would come out of their sockets, and her hands began to slip due to the perspiration pouring from her palms.

'Lance!' she cried, fearing she would be buried in the sand forever. Or at least until some future archaeologist found her there and probably mistook her for some Egyptian princess.

'Hold tight!' he called.

'I'm trying . . . '

'Prepare yourself,' he said, before

suddenly letting go with one hand whilst pulling her upwards with the other, so that his free hand caught her elbow instead. 'One more,' he said, his breath coming in bursts from the exertion. He swung her upwards again, this time catching her by her armpits. She wrapped her arms around his neck.

He very quickly hoisted her up into the chamber above. It was about six feet high, and opened out into the sunlight. They climbed the rocky walls for what seemed like ages. When they finally came out into the bright sunlight, they found they were in a small aperture behind the crown of one of the statues of Ramses on the façade of the temple.

'Do you think we just did our stint of Purgatory?' Lance asked with a grin.

'I certainly hope so!'

They climbed down, grateful to feel the solid ground below their feet. The other tourists watched with interest before deciding they had other things to do.

'We did it!' Nadine said. Lance picked her up and spun her around. 'I need a drink,' she added when they had calmed down.

'Yeah, me too. Come on, back to the boat.'

For a brief moment, Nadine was sure she saw the old Arab man who had been following them around, but he disappeared into the shade of the temple and she did not want to go after him in case it was someone else. Besides, she was too exhausted from her exertions. She wanted a bathe and a good strong drink, even if that drink was only hot, sweet tea.

'That was fun,' she said to Lance. 'I think I get it now. Why you do all this.'

'You haven't seen the half of it,' he said.

Only when they reached the boat did Nadine start to feel guilty for her enjoyment of the adventure. Poor Prince Ari was dead, possibly by suicide — and here they were, celebrating. She affected a more serious expression, as did Lance, before going to bathe and then joining the other tourists for dinner.

It was perhaps lucky for Nadine and Lance that everyone was so preoccupied with the prince that no one asked what they had been up to.

'Where is Miss Bentley?' the countess asked Nadine, when she sat down at their usual table.

'I've no idea. Is she not on the boat?'

'No, she left not long after you and Mr Smith, and said she intended to join you.'

Nadine shook her head. 'We didn't see her.' She could hardly explain that where they had been, Valerie Bentley could not possibly have followed. 'Perhaps she went to the smaller temple and missed us. I'm sure she'll be along soon. How are you feeling, Countess? Did you enjoy your rest?'

'Yes, thank you, Nadine. I shall be glad when we leave this place and move on. It has been most solemn today.'

'It's not surprising, given what

happened to the prince,' Nadine said, with a pang of shame. She had not given him much thought at all in the past few hours. She really was beginning to understand what drove both Lance and her father to do what they did. The buzz from the excitement could easily become an addiction.

Lance was once again sitting with the Suttons. She glanced across and waved, but he looked very bored. Miss Sutton was talking about some tour they had been on to South America, learning about Aztec history, whilst Mr Sutton was his usual silent self.

'I've just been saying,' the countess said to the other guests, 'that Miss Bentley will miss her dinner if she is not careful.'

'I wonder where she can be,' Miss Sutton said. 'She was supposed to be meeting Miss Middleton and Mr Smith.'

'Yes, I've just been telling Nadine that. She claims they have not seen her.'

'We didn't see her,' said Lance. 'But

it's a big complex. We could easily have missed her.'

'We could ask the stewards to save her something,' Nadine suggested.

Everyone agreed that was a good idea. It relieved everyone of guilt for not waiting to eat. Even abroad, the British niceties must be maintained.

As the night wore on, and they moved to the salon, the tourists became more concerned.

'Still no sign of Miss Bentley,' said Miss Sutton. She had walked across to the sofa under the window, where Nadine sat sewing one of the countess's shawls. Miss Sutton looked out into the night. The temple complex was lit up, and some tourists still lingered, due to it being a very pretty sight and much cooler than in the heat of the day.

'Perhaps we should go and look,' Nadine suggested. 'She may not have realised what time it is.'

'I hardly think so,' the countess called from the bridge table where she, the count, Mr Sutton and Mr Hardcastle were playing. 'You cannot go out there, Nadine. It's getting dark.'

'Not really our concern,' said Mr Hardcastle. 'Grown woman and all that.'

'After what has happened to the prince, we ought to be more concerned,' Nadine reminded him.

'Yes, yes. Suppose so. I'll get my man Devon on it. Devon.' Mr Hardcastle snapped his fingers and Devon, who had been sitting near the bar, came dashing over.

'Yes, Mr Hardcastle.'

'Go and tell the stewards that Miss Bentley has not returned for dinner and we're all worried about her. You tell those Egyptian Johnnies that we worry about our young ladies and want them safe.'

Nadine rolled her eyes at Hardcastle's sudden change of tune, and got up to leave the salon. Lance was standing out on the deck, smoking a cigarette and looking towards the temple. 'It's hard to believe what's hidden behind that façade,' he said to her as she approached him.

'Valerie Bentley hasn't come back yet,' she said, acknowledging his words with a brief nod. 'I'm worried. Regardless of what the countess says, I'm going to go over to the temple and see if I can find her. That old Arab was there today, I'm sure of it. He's followed us since the train to Cairo.'

'I'll come with you.' Lance threw his cigarette into the lake.

They searched the complex for over an hour, but there was no sign of Valerie. It was nearly ten o'clock before they returned to the boat and asked if she had come back. The others answered in the negative.

'We should search her cabin,' Nadine suggested. 'She might have left a clue.'

'I'm sure we should not, Nadine,' the countess chided, whilst engrossed in the cards she held in her hand. 'Really, child, you're not a detective.' She also had changed her tune since earlier in the day, but Nadine was becoming used to the countess's contradictory behaviour. Valerie Bentley was beneath the countess's notice: ergo she did not really care what happened to her. The only reason she had raised the issue was because it was what one was expected to do. Having mentioned the girl, the countess quickly grew bored with the subject. 'Let the count deal with it. Dear?' She turned to her husband. 'Will you?'

'Of course, my love. But I will take Nadine with me, as I do not think it would be proper for a man of my age to go rummaging through Miss Bentley's belongings.' He got up and winked at Nadine, who followed him gratefully.

They had to ask a steward to unlock Valerie's door, and at first he was resistant. 'It is an invasion of the young lady's privacy,' he said, not unreasonably. 'We must protect our guests.'

'We're concerned about her,' Nadine stressed as politely as she could. 'We know it's an imposition, and we wouldn't ask otherwise.'

The count spoke to the steward in his own language and that seemed to do the trick. A few seconds later the door was opened.

Nadine flicked on the light and went in. 'But . . . ' Her voice died away.

The room was as if it had never been slept in. She went to the wardrobe and looked inside, but everything had gone. All the cupboard drawers were empty. Any signs that Valerie might have slept in that room or used its facilities had been eradicated. It was made up ready for the next guest.

'This is impossible.' She turned to the count. 'She's just gone, disappeared. All her clothes. Everything. Someone must have helped her, yet the stewards are denying everything. Someone must have seen her leave.'

The count shrugged. 'Then there is nothing we can do,' he said. 'Miss Bentley has obviously left of her own accord.'

'Or she's dead,' Nadine said, her voice rising in panic. 'Someone has done something to her.'

'Nadine, dear girl. Are you familiar with Occam's Razor?'

'No.'

'It says that when you have eliminated all other possibilities, the simplest explanation must be the correct one. Put quite simply, Miss Bentley has decided to leave the cruise, and has taken all her belongings with her. I am sure people do that all the time.' The count spoke to the steward in Arabic again.

'Yes, yes, indeed,' said the steward. 'Sometimes people just disappear. There is nothing we can do when they decide to leave.'

'One of your staff must have helped her off with her bags,' Nadine said. 'Yet you say you don't know what happened.'

'Perhaps she wanted her departure to be kept private,' the count said pointedly.

'She did not inform us she was leaving, Count Chlomsky,' said the steward. 'I am sorry, Miss Middleton, but that is the truth.'

'The prince is dead and now a woman is missing,' Nadine protested. 'Can't you see a problem with that?'

'Are you suggesting that Miss Bentley killed the prince?' asked the count.

'What? No. No, not at all. Why would she?'

'Come.' The count held out his hand to Nadine. 'We have done all we can, but we cannot prevent a grown woman from leaving the boat if that is what she wanted to do.'

'Someone helped her,' Nadine repeated as they went back to the salon. 'Someone must have. She couldn't have got all her luggage off the boat without someone noticing.'

The rest of the tourists in the salon were mildly curious about Valerie's disappearance, in the way people are when they've run out of anything else to discuss, having spent so long in each other's company. Even the prince's death had not consumed them for very long, on account of no one really knowing him. It was less of a nine-day wonder, and more of a nine-minute one. The fact that Valerie was English made her marginally more interesting to her fellow passengers.

'Did no one see her take her luggage?' Nadine asked. 'Or did you see anyone taking luggage off the boat?'

'Well, yes,' said Miss Sutton. She and her brother were playing backgammon. 'Several passengers disembarked today. They weren't in our party, but I did overhear one of them saying that they felt the death of the prince would bring bad luck to the boat. It's all poppycock. People fall overboard on these trips all the time. I heard of one man who was eaten by a crocodile.'

'So Valerie's luggage could have been taken off with the other passengers', Nadine mused. 'And no one would have noticed because one pile of suitcases looks very much like another.'

'It isn't our concern, child,' the countess said. 'So please do stop talking about it. I know you and the young lady got on well, but these holiday friendships never last. No offence to anyone . . . ' She waved her arm to encompass the whole salon. ' . . . but I'm sure I shall forget you all five minutes after I arrive back in Britain.'

'Not me, I hope,' the count said mildly.

'Oh, Count, you know what I mean.' The countess laughed. 'He's just being silly.'

Nadine excused herself, claiming exhaustion. It was not entirely untrue. It had been a gruelling day, with one thing and another.

She felt hurt that Valerie had not said goodbye to her. They had been friends, and even if it was only one of those transient acquaintanceships, a farewell would have been polite.

To help take her mind off things, Nadine decided to look through her father's journal again and re-read some of the clues. There were two more keys left to find, and it would help to throw herself into that rather than worry about a woman who could not even be bothered to leave a note.

She went to her newest hiding place — she changed it every day, and on this occasion had taped the key behind the mirror in her bathroom — and reached in to get it, only to find that it had gone.

Nadine went out onto the deck, as if she thought she might catch the thief. She saw nothing but two lovers locked together in a tight embrace. As she turned back into her cabin, they moved apart, and she saw that it was Miss Sutton and her brother.

10

Eventually they were allowed to leave Abu Simbel, and the boat sailed on to Wadi Halfa. In doing so they crossed the border into the Sudan and Upper Nubia.

Wadi Halfa was a relatively new town, established in the nineteenth century. However, there were many ancient monuments in the area, and it was at this point that Nadine decided to leave the countess and travel onwards to Semna. She had made notes of her father's journal, so hoped she had enough to be going on with.

She had planned to just leave, but Valerie's behaviour had shown her how impolite that would be, so she went to see the countess on the morning after they arrived at the Wadi Halfa Rail Road Hotel.

'I'm afraid I must resign,' she said.

'Resign? But why, child?' The countess was lying back in her bed, dressed in a fine silk negligee. On a younger woman it might have been attractive. On the elderly, wrinkled countess it looked like a shroud. It gave Nadine a pang to realise that the old woman might not be around much longer, and she had not exactly been the best of secretaries to her.

'I have things I need to do. I'm sorry to leave you, but I only ever wanted to get this far.'

'You can't just leave. Really, it's most inconvenient. Clementine will be very put out when I write and tell her.'

'Aunt Clementine knows what I plan to do. She's known all along.'

'Let the girl go, Victoria,' said the count, coming in from the bathroom. He was wearing a royal blue dressing gown. 'I have explained it to you.'

Nadine frowned. What did the count know of her quest?

'Did you, Count? I don't remember.' The countess also frowned. 'It's most inconvenient, and when my memoirs are nearly complete. I would not have minded if you'd married the prince. At least then I can say that I have saved you from disgrace.'

'I'm not in disgrace,' Nadine said.

'Well . . . with your father being a charlatan . . . '

'My father was not a charlatan; and even if he was, I am not. People must judge me as they find me, not by my father.' Nadine began to feel somewhat hot under the collar. 'Believe me, Countess, over the past week I have seen things that defy logic. I have . . . ' Nadine faltered. She was in danger of giving away all her secrets. She was also feeling guilty now that the time had come for her to go. Nadine recognised the countess as a lonely old woman who, apart from her husband, had very few other friends. Her occasionally waspish behaviour might be a reason for that, but Nadine believed that she meant well. 'I'm sorry, truly I am. If I am able to complete my quest, I will come back and help you with your memoirs, I promise.'

'I might have found another girl by then.'

'That's fair enough. I don't expect you to wait for me.'

'I'm sure she will wait,' said the count, his eyes twinkling with their usual kindness. 'We have discussed this, dearest.'

Again, Nadine wondered how much the count knew. Had Aunt Clementine told him? Or was his interest purely personal? He was a funny little man. Kind, yes; but he was also much shrewder than his diffident manner suggested. He was said to have been a double agent in the past, and some still questioned his loyalties. He was the consummate politician, able to agree with everyone at once whilst offending no one.

'I'll leave straight away,' Nadine said. 'I've asked the hotel to store my luggage. I won't take everything with me. Goodbye, Countess Chlomsky.

Count Chlomsky. Thank you both for everything.' She almost curtseyed but thought better of it.

'Remember, Nadine,' said the count, 'if you ever need any help, you know where to find us.'

'That's very kind, thank you.'

Nadine left them then, as she was in danger of becoming emotional. It was not that she had any great affection for the countess, who had sometimes been quite a difficult employer (Nadine conceded she had not been the best employee, either), but she felt that she was cutting ties with civilisation and her only hope of getting out of Egypt alive.

When she went to the reception to check out of the hotel, the concierge handed her a note. 'For you, Miss Middleton.'

She opened it eagerly and found it was a message from Valerie Bentley.

Dear Nadine,
I am so sorry I left without saying goodbye. You have been a good

friend and companion. I just wanted you to know that I am very happy. Happier than I have ever been. I doubt we shall ever meet again, so I wish you all the love and happiness in the world.
Your friend,
Valerie Bentley

Though it was unlikely they would meet again, seeing it written down concerned Nadine. Normally, fellow travellers made promises to meet up again, even if they did not intend to keep them. It was as if Valerie intended to fall off the face of the earth. Why would she do that? Had she had some hand in the prince's death? If the authorities had any suspicions, they would not have let her leave. The whole thing about the prince killing himself and Valerie disappearing on the same day was perplexing. But the question Nadine really asked was whether it had anything to do with her own quest.

'I've got the horses. Are you ready?'

Nadine turned to see Lance standing in the hotel doorway. She frowned again. She had decided to trust him, yet something in her heart held her back from admitting her true feelings. They had not kissed since the night of the sandstorm. It had been impossible to find time alone on the boat, and she had not felt comfortable enough with him to invite him into her cabin.

Yet seeing him standing there, wearing a leather jacket, with a bullwhip hanging from his belt and a black fedora on his head, aroused her in ways she had never experienced. He exuded masculinity from every pore, and it made her feel rather small and girly. She would have to keep her wits about her if she was going to prevent this man from stealing the stone right from under her nose. One more kiss and she might just hand it to him without argument. She only hoped she would not behave that pathetically.

'Ready,' she said, standing up tall and determined not to give in to weakness where Lancaster Smith was concerned. Temperance was the next virtue to be uncovered, and Nadine intended to adhere to it, regardless of the storm raging in her mind and body.

'You off?' a voice bellowed from the foyer.

'Yes, Mr Hardcastle,' Nadine said. 'We're going exploring. There are some interesting old forts in the area.' That was not strictly untrue.

'Odd thing. Young gal going getting all muddy and dirty.'

'I enjoy it.' That much was true. Nadine had never imagined archaeology to be so exciting. Her father's other colleagues had been rather dry and dull, spending most of their time in the dusty archives of the British Museum.

'Rather you than me. Ah, Miss Sutton. I don't suppose you're going to go delving in old ruins.'

'Certainly not,' said Miss Sutton. 'My brother and I intend to relax before taking the steamer back to Cairo.'

Nadine smiled awkwardly. She could

not get the image of Miss Sutton and her brother kissing out of her head. She tried to tell herself it was their business, but it still made her cringe inwardly. It was a good job she would never see them again. Sometimes it really was best not to know too much about people.

'What's going on there?' Lance asked, as they rode away from the town. 'You actually blushed when you saw Miss Sutton.'

'I saw her kissing her brother,' Nadine blurted out. It was such a relief to be able to tell someone apart from Aunt Clementine, who had heard about it, along with news of the other guests, in one of Nadine's regular letters. The only thing Nadine had not told her was about the quest for the keys and the stone. It did not do for Aunt Clementine to know everything that was happening, even if she had known Nadine's real reason for coming to Egypt.

'What?' Lance laughed incredulously.

'I mean, kissing. Properly kissing. As lovers do. I always thought there was something strange about them. He hardly ever speaks, and she makes the decisions for them all the time.'

'Hmm.' Lance looked into the distance, yet to Nadine he appeared lost in a dream world. He scratched his cheek thoughtfully.

'She asked a lot of questions about you and the other passengers too, now I come to think of it,' Nadine said. 'The night I was accosted in Cairo. I wonder if she led me into a trap.'

'They don't look much alike,' Lance said.

'No, but brothers and sisters don't always, do they? Oh, are you saying they're not brother and sister?'

'Maybe. If they're not married, it could be the only way they could travel without causing a scandal was as siblings.'

'That makes sense; and, I have to say, is more palatable than the alternative,' Nadine said with a smile. She suddenly felt lighter. 'Of course, that's it. They're lovers but can only travel as brother and sister. Maybe she has a husband or he has a wife. Or they both have spouses.'

'And you think adultery is better than incest?'

'Oh God, yes! Admittedly, it's not nice, and very hard on the other party, but at least it's sort of normal. So that's what they are. Secret lovers. Thank goodness we solved that mystery. Onward to Semna and our next adventure!'

Nadine tapped her horse with her feet and set off into the distance, leaving Lance to catch up.

They rode for fifteen miles along the bank of the Nile, until they reached the Second Cataract. The Nile Cataracts were where the water was shallower and rockier, leading to rushing water or rapids. The going was dangerous for boats, but the sparkling water made the surrounding air somewhat fresher.

There had been three forts in Semna. One in the East, one in the

West and one in the South. The forts were built to prevent the nomadic tribes interfering with the goods produced in southern Nubia. The South Fort had been discovered in the nineteen-twenties, but had not yet been excavated. It was to this fort they travelled, reasoning that all its secrets had not yet been discovered, unlike the others'.

When they reached the area where the fort was situated, they jumped down off their horses and drank some of the water from their canteens.

'Do you want to eat?' Lance asked Nadine. They had also packed bread, fruit and wine.

'No, not yet. I'm too excited.' Nadine stood on the banks of the Nile looking out at the rushing water. It all seemed far more dramatic than the sedate waters down which they had travelled further north. She supposed this was why the steamers did not come this far.

'It's a wonderful country,' she said to Lance. 'So much history, and yet you feel as though it's still happening. Cleopatra might have stood in this very spot thousands of years ago . . . five minutes ago . . . Lance?'

'What?' He stood next to her looking out over the river.

'How did the scales at Abu Simbel know that we were speaking? Or that we were even saying the right things?'

'I don't know. Maybe it was some sort of phonic trick. If you say the right words at the right pitch, it activates some machinery behind the wall. Like kinetic energy.'

'Is that possible?'

'Why not? If you blow on a candle it usually goes out, but if you blew it in the right direction — or the wrong direction, if you prefer — the flame could set fire to the drapes and the whole house would go up. You're not saying it was magic, are you?'

'I think it was less magic and more to do with spirituality.'

'Like God was listening?' Lance raised an eyebrow. 'I don't know if I even believe in God. Either one god or several.'

'Don't you? Yet you encouraged me to say my reverse confessions.'

'It was worth a try, and it worked, for whatever reason. Sometimes you just don't question these things.'

'You're a scientist!' Nadine turned to him. 'You're supposed to question.'

'Even scientists don't have all the answers. If we did, then we'd have nothing else to do. The fun is in searching for the answers. Even then, we have to allow for the things we don't know and might never know. Think about it. If an ancient Egyptian saw a modern motor car, he would think it was magic. We only know it's not because we know how it was invented by Henry Ford. So why can't it work the other way? Why can't the Egyptians have invented something — some way of tipping those scales — that we don't know about because we know nothing of the invention that makes it happen? Ergo, it looks like magic. This is what your father believed, Nadine. That there was a lot of stuff we don't know about because the secrets behind the inventions have been lost to time.'

'What about seeing the future?' Nadine asked. 'No machine could ever do that.'

'You only say that because such a machine hasn't been invented yet. Meteorologists can tell us what the weather is going to be like. If you read the papers at the moment, you can see that all signs are leading to war. In nineteen hundred and one, the *Antikythera mechanism* was discovered. It was a machine that could predict astrological positions. Now, with the computers that scientists use, it's possible that all these things could be fed into a giant machine, and that machine predict the likely outcomes of any given event. That's telling the future, Nadine.'

'But we're not talking about a machine guessing what might happen, Lance, with no real certainty of the outcome. Even meteorologists get it wrong. The Eye of the Storm is a jewel, not a machine.'

'So? Maybe the Egyptians found a way to miniaturise the mechanism. Some writers believe that computing machines will eventually become smaller. Who's to say they haven't been in the past, but we just don't recognise them because they're nothing like we expect? You're looking at me as if I'm crazy; yet your father believed all these things, and people said *he* was crazy.'

'*You* said he was crazy . . . '

'Because he asked me to. Because he saw how dangerous the Eye could be.'

'So why are we looking for it?' Nadine asked.

'You're determined to find it, and I'm determined to take care of you until you do.'

'I don't need you to take care of me, Lance.'

'Shall I leave?' He moved closer to her.

'No . . . no, I'm not saying that. I like having you here. I like sharing all this with you . . . Just don't treat me like some helpless little woman, because I'm not.'

He stroked her cheek. 'Pity, because I kinda like saving you.'

'Maybe *I'll* save *you*.'

'That'd be just as good.'

'Shall we find this other key?' Nadine made to step back, but he caught her around the waist and pulled her to him, his mouth covering hers. They stayed locked like that for what seemed an age, yet was over far too soon.

'Forget it, Nadine,' he murmured against her cheek. 'There are things happening that you don't know about. We don't have to get caught up in any of it. Let's just go home and have babies and be happy.'

'Are you asking me to marry you?'

'Yes.'

'Why?'

'I'd have thought that was obvious. I love you and you love me.'

'I don't.' She did not sound convincing even to herself.

'You don't?'

'No.'

'You kiss me as if you love me.'

'Loving someone means trusting them. I'm not sure if I can trust you, Lance.'

'I'm asking you to give the whole quest up and come home with me. How can that be untrustworthy?' Lance pulled away from her and looked her straight in the eye.

'You're trying to stall me. Or put me off altogether. Perhaps so you can go and find the Eye of the Storm yourself whilst I'm busy back at home, being barefoot and pregnant. That's what my dad did to my mother. He saved all his adventures for when he was away from her, instead of joining her in the biggest, scariest adventure there is: being a husband and a father. He spent all his life running away from us. I don't want to be left behind, Lance. So are you with me or not?'

'I'm with you. Always.'

'Good. Let's go and find this key.'

'So that's a definite no to marriage?'

'It's a definite no to being left at home. If you come up with a better offer, I'm ready to listen.' With her heart hammering madly, Nadine turned away and pulled a map out of her rucksack, determined to look business-like despite her emotions being in turmoil. She was an idiot. She should have just said yes! What if he didn't ask again? She let him know none of this tumult, determined to remain calm and collected. 'Now, where is this fort? And how do we get into it?'

'You really are impossible, woman!'

'I know. It makes me adorable, doesn't it?' She turned and winked at him.

'Unfortunately for me, yes.'

It took them some time to work out where the outline of the fort was. There were a few rocks scattered around — which, when they looked again, they realised were set in some sort of formation. The fort had been square, but there were other buildings around it, including a church, houses, and a cemetery.

'Temperance was the next virtue on Dad's list,' Nadine said. 'It has quite a few symbols associated with it, including a wheel, bridle and reins, fish, cups, two wine jugs . . . I'm guessing that the Eye of the Storm must have been hidden by Christians, as most of the symbols we've found are from Judeo-Christian mythology rather than Egyptian.'

'Now you're thinking like an archaeologist, and you're probably right. There was quite a large Christian settlement in Egypt at one time,' Lance explained. 'The Catholic Church looks upon fortune-telling with distrust. The Eye must have scared those early Christians to death. It makes sense that they went to such lengths to hide it.'

'Then left easy clues so we knew where it was . . . '

'They probably thought it might

come in handy one day. Never say never.'

They searched each stone and rock in turn, using a trowel and a brush to work around them, but none bore the symbols of temperance or any of the other virtues. 'It's hopeless,' Nadine groaned after several hours. 'Like looking for the proverbial needle in a haystack.' She went back to the river bank to collect her thoughts. The heat from the sun seared through her clothes, making her feel hot and heavy. This was the part of archaeology she could easily do without. The legwork. Or brushwork, as the case may be. No wonder European archaeologists paid the locals to do all that for them.

Lance followed her and put his hands on her shoulder, massaging her neck muscles. 'Do you still think they made it too easy?' he asked.

She laughed, but there was little humour in it. 'No, perhaps not . . . ' She looked down at the river, feeling forlorn and totally fed up. The bottom was filled with various debris, some of which had been washed down from the upper part of the Nile. There were even cigarette packets and old shoes. 'Oh, look. Someone has thrown an old pewter jug into the river. I don't suppose they care if it's ancient or not. Such artefacts are probably ten a penny around here.'

She gingerly stepped into the shallowest part of the river and reached down to lift up the pot.

'Careful, or a sudden squall might pull you under,' Lance warned.

'It's stuck . . . I . . . ' Nadine tugged hard and the pot came away. Suddenly there was a *glug glug* sound and the waters became a swirling mass, like a bath emptying down the plughole. She had time to call out, 'Lance!' before her foot got caught in the tempest and she felt herself being sucked downwards.

A hand grabbed hers, and both Nadine and Lance slid down a long, wet and winding tunnel, being tossed this way and that, and occasionally spinning around the edge of the flume so that they no longer knew what was up or down. Luckily, the water was beneath their bodies, so they could still breathe. For a short time there was some light above them, but that soon disappeared. Nadine had time to wonder if the whirlpool had closed up after them, putting the jug back in place.

The deeper they went, the darker it became, until they could see nothing and had no idea where they were heading or whether they were even going to land safely. At first they both squealed, as one would on a roller-coaster, but even that seemed redundant when they just kept going and going.

'How long do you think this thing is?' Nadine called to Lance.

'A couple of miles at least,' Lance called back. 'Don't ask me what direction. We could be under the Nile or on our way back to Wadi Halfa!'

'It's quite fun, though, isn't it?' Nadine said.

'If you like being wet and blind, yeah, it's great.'

'Spoilsport!'

They finally landed on a pile of mud, which covered their already-soaked clothing.

'Oh, look,' Nadine said, standing up. 'Another chamber. How did they manage to dig so deep? And where is all the light coming from?'

'How did people manage to move those enormous stones to Stonehenge? How did they build the pyramids?' Lance asked. 'Human resourcefulness knows no bounds. I'm guessing the tunnel that led us here is a natural phenomenon that they've utilised for the purpose. Like an enormous pot-hole. What's next on our list of virtues?'

'Temperance. So I'm guessing our self-restraint is going to be tested. But how?'

Nadine walked to the centre of the chamber and looked around. There was a plinth in the middle, and on it stood two jugs. 'Look here. There's water in one of these, and what looks like wine in the other. That goes with the next clue: '*Mix water with the wine to reach the divine . . .* ' The jug with the water was three-quarters full, and the jug with the wine was full to the brim.

'So I'm guessing we have to mix the two liquids together. That's not too difficult.' Lance reached for one of the jugs.'

'Wait!' Nadine said. 'It's not going to be that easy.' She touched the plinth and it wobbled beneath her hand. At the same time, the liquids in the jugs swayed. 'If we spill any, I think this plinth is going to move and maybe open up another dark pit for us. These people really like their pits.'

'It's their idea of hell, I guess,' Lance agreed. 'So we drink some of the wine, tip the rest into the water and . . . '

'Why the wine?' Nadine asked. 'Why not the water?'

'There's more wine than water. We can't add water to the wine. It will tip over the brim. But we can add wine to the water. They still have to balance. The only way to do that is drink some of the wine, and then tip enough of the rest into the water so that the jugs stay the same weight or level.'

'The key word is temperance, Lance. If we drink the wine, then we're not being temperate. I say we drink none of the wine, but we add some of it into the water. That way each jug will hold the same amount. But that's too easy and how can we measure it perfectly? One drop too many and we don't know what will happen. Is it me, or is it warm in here?'

Nadine had not noticed the heat until then, but once she did, it quickly became overpowering. Her already-damp clothes stuck to her, causing her skin to feel itchy. A bead of sweat dripped from her forehead onto one of her eyelashes.

'Lance . . . '

'Yeah, you're right.' He took off his hat and rubbed his own forehead. 'It's like a sauna in here. There must be a heat source somewhere.'

'And it's getting warmer. What time is it?'

Lance looked at his watch. 'Noon.'

'The sun will be at its highest then. But how can it reach down here?' Nadine held her hand up. 'No, don't tell me. Something we didn't know they invented. Ouch.' She quickly hopped from one foot to another. 'The floor is getting hotter.'

'Let's get higher,' Lance said. 'Come on, back to the mud. It has cooling properties.'

The mud only cooled them for a short time as the whole chamber became like a furnace. 'I need a drink,' Nadine said, reaching to her belt for her flask. It was gone. She remembered taking a sip of water by the river, but couldn't recall if she had put the flask down. For all she knew, it had come off in the flume. 'Oh no! Do you have any water left?'

'No. I left mine on my horse.'

'That was stupid. What if the horse ran away?'

'And your flask is where, exactly?'

'Okay, point taken.'

'The way I see it, we're supposed to drink the water from the jug,' Lance said. 'That's the test. That's why it's so darn hot.'

'If we do that . . . '

'Then the plinth will be unstable and we don't know what comes next.'

'What if it doesn't become unstable? What if the test was to see if we'd drink the wine? So by drinking the water, we're being restrained.'

'Do you wanna test it?'

'Not really.' Nadine's shoulders slumped. 'If the test is restraint, for all we know we're not supposed to drink any of it. But that doesn't make sense either.' She wiped her neck and undid a couple of buttons on her shirt, exposing the lacy edge of her bra.

Lance had undone his shirt too. She could see a fine mass of dark hair poking out from the top. Their eyes met, and all thoughts of thirst died away to be replaced by an overpowering hunger. All she could think of was running her hands through the hairs on his chest.

'Lance . . . ' she whispered, closing her eyes. The heat came from within them now, making them forget everything else.

'What, honey?' he asked in a silky voice.

'I don't think it's our thirst they're expecting us to quench in this heat.'

'I've just been thinking the same . . . '

'So we mustn't give in, right?' Despite her words, Nadine edged closer to him.

'No, not at all. I'm pretty resolute.' He moved closer to her.

'Nobody really wants to make love on a pile of mud anyway.' Closer and closer, they came together.

'Nope. Can't think of anything worse.' Their lips were only a couple of millimetres apart.

'On the other hand,' Nadine said,

'we'd be cooler if we took all our clothes off.'

'Can't argue with that logic. You're a very clever woman, Nadine Middleton.'

'You're only saying that because you want me to be naked.'

'I have to admit, I've given it some thought.'

'Lance?'

'What, darling?'

'Why did you turn me down five years ago?'

'You were only seventeen. In my country, men go to prison for that. I know you have slightly different rules in Britain, but I can't change the way I think.'

'So it wasn't because I was repugnant to you?'

'You definitely weren't repugnant. You couldn't be, even if you tried. You're beautiful and funny and clever. You're probably the worst secretary in the world, but I don't need any typing done anyway.'

She laughed. 'I'm glad to hear it. I don't really feel like typing right now.'

She put her hand on his shoulder. 'Funny how you can forget about the mud, isn't it?'

'Yeah . . . ' Their lips were a fraction off kissing when Lance jumped up and moved away from her, leaving her feeling bereft. 'There must be another water source here somewhere. How else does the jug keep being replenished with fresh water? I bet it's like the feathers at the other place. There'll be some cave above where the water is filtered from the Nile. It doesn't explain how the jug is only three-quarters full, but . . . What? Why are you looking at me like that, Nadine?'

'You just said I wasn't repugnant.'

'You're not, but when I make love to you . . . and believe me, I will one day . . . it won't be in some muddy old cave where some ancient sadists are playing mind games with us. Come on, Nadine, you said it yourself. Restraint is the order of the day.'

She stood up, her lips set in a pout. 'Okay, but you just lost your only chance with me.' She did not really mean it, but frustration was making her crotchety.

He winked. 'We'll see.' She hated that he seemed to know what she was really thinking.

'We'd better start looking,' she started to say, but her foot caught on something in the mud and she almost tripped up. 'Look, Lance, it's the jug I saw in the river. Or one very much like it.'

'I guess it fell down the hole with us.'

'But don't you see? It's like we used to do at school, where we had to move liquid between different containers. Did you do that in America? This jug is a fraction of the size of the others. We fill this with water, which we drink, and then we replace that water in the jug with the wine. Or something . . . Mathematics was never my strong point. My guess is that the liquids will then be the same volume and the plinth won't move. It doesn't explain why the fact they're not balanced now doesn't make the plinth move; but, as you say, it's all invention-y stuff we don't even know about.'

'The test is not in the balance,' Lance suggested. 'It's in working out how it's done.'

'Yes! Shall we try?' Nadine hesitated. There was no guarantee that even her way was correct.

'I've run out of other ideas. Oh, just one thing.'

'What's that?'

'Please button up your blouse. I'm not as restrained as I thought I was.'

Nadine grinned. 'Good.' She went to the plinth. 'Come here,' she said to Lance. 'You'd better stay close to me. We don't know where this is going to take us next. We should brace ourselves for another fall.'

She filled the jug with water and they both took a drink. The water was a bit tepid, but it did seem fairly fresh. Then Nadine filled the smaller jug with wine and poured that into the water. As she had believed, both of the jugs finally held the same volume of fluid.

They waited, expecting to be swept away, but instead the stone plinth rolled back and revealed a staircase leading downwards. They began to walk down, but Nadine stopped. 'Did you hear something? The water is rushing down the flume again.'

They turned and looked back towards the pile of mud, expecting to see someone, but there was no one there.

'Never mind,' said Lance. 'Let's not hang around.'

They went down the dimly-lit staircase, and at the bottom found another set of stairs leading upwards. That set was spiral and had hundreds of steps. By the time they reached the top, they were exhausted and thirsty again, but at least it was cooler. There was an old wooden door at the top. As it was a bit stiff, they pushed it together, and it opened out into a room that was lit with thousands of candles. It had an altar at the end. There were stained glass windows, but no light came from them as they were buried, on the outside, in sand. It reminded Nadine of a glass swan her grandmother had bought at the seaside, which was filled with different colours of sand.

'It's a church!' Nadine exclaimed.

'And a well-maintained one, by the look of things,' said Lance.

'You mean someone comes here?'

'Yep. Unless another invention we haven't found yet is the everlasting candle.'

'We have electric light bulbs. That's like an everlasting candle.'

'These are real candles.'

They walked up to the altar, on which were three silver goblets. Above the altar, set into four recesses, were statues depicting the four cardinal virtues. Prudence was shown as a beautiful woman, looking into a mirror which had a snake wrapped around it. Justice held a set of scales in one hand and the sword of truth in another. Temperance held two jugs, spilling fluid from one to the other. Fortitude wore a breastplate and fought with a lion.

'So where is the key?' Nadine said, not really asking Lance. He would have no better idea than her.

'It said *mix water with the wine to reach the divine*,' Lance said, turning back to the goblets. 'Somehow I don't think that just applied to the water in the chamber downstairs.' He pointed to the goblets. 'They've all got fluid in them. I'm guessing that one of them is wine and water and we have to drink it.'

Nadine looked at each goblet in turn. 'They all look the same.'

'They won't be.'

'Do you think one of them might be poisonous?'

'I'd bet my life on it.'

'Why don't we find out?' said a voice from behind them.

They spun around to see Hardcastle and his secretary, Devon, standing at the door. Both men held guns, which were pointed directly at Nadine and Lance.

11

Several other men followed Mr. Hard-castle and Devon through the entrance door. They were attired in the black uniforms of the German SS.

'Thank you for leading us this far, Miss Middleton,' said Hardcastle.

'You're working with the Germans,' Nadine said, aware she was stating the obvious.

'I have a liking for Mr. Hitler,' Hardcastle confessed. 'He's a man with sound ideas.'

'Persecuting a whole race because of their religion,' Nadine scoffed. 'You call that a good idea?'

'I don't care about that. What are a few lives to me? I've been promised a weapons contract for this whole damn war, and as much money and research as I want.'

'You're a traitor to your country!'

'I'm a realist. And a capitalist.'

'We're wasting time,' Devon said. 'You don't have to explain yourself to them.'

'True,' Hardcastle agreed. 'Let's find out which goblet holds the key, shall we? You . . . ' He waved his gun at Lance. 'Drink from the middle one.'

'Why drink it?' asked Lance. 'We could just tip them out.'

Nadine instinctively knew that it was not going to be that easy. Nothing else about their quest had been. They had mixed water and wine in the other chamber. Now they had to work out which goblet held the divine. Or the key, as the case might be.

'Besides,' Lance continued, 'you don't want to kill us. We know where to go next.'

Hardcastle thought about it for a moment.

'We don't need them,' Devon said.

'We might,' Hardcastle insisted. 'Well, one of them, and my money is on him. He's the archaeologist. She's just a secretary; and not even a very good one, according to the countess.' He turned his gun on Nadine. 'Drink from the middle goblet.'

'No,' Nadine protested.

'She won't do it,' Lance said.

'Do it!' Devon barked. He looked from Lance to Nadine, then back again, and grinned, showing pointed canines. 'Drink the wine or I will shoot your lover.' He turned his gun on Lance.

Nadine gazed at Lance with wide eyes. If she did not drink, he would be dead. If she did drink, she might die. She knew then that she loved him more than life itself, and would rather he go on living.

She stepped forward and picked up the middle goblet, raising it to her lips. Her hands trembled, and she could almost taste death even before she drank the first sip of wine. She almost gagged on the first mouthful, but was relieved to find it tasted like ordinary sacramental wine.

She was halfway down the goblet

when an impatient Hardcastle swiped it from her hands and gave it to one of the soldiers. 'Drink the rest,' he said. 'I don't trust her not to hide the key away somehow.'

The young man took the goblet from Hardcastle and knocked back the remains. He looked into the cup, perplexed. 'Nothing,' he said.

'What?' Hardcastle took the goblet and looked inside. 'Where is it?'

Suddenly the soldier put his hand to his throat and started gagging.

What happened next would stay with Nadine forever, and haunt her worst nightmares. The young man's face became inflamed, as did his hands and the skin of his throat. He scratched at his skin as if trying to put out a fire. It seemed like he was catching fire from the inside out, before his body burst into flames and his tortured screams rang throughout the church. The screaming went on incessantly, until he crumpled to the floor and died.

The other soldiers looked on in

horror. Nadine felt sorry for them, and for the young man who had died. Something, or more likely someone, had steered them in the wrong direction. Being young, they probably believed all the things Hitler said. Or perhaps they were just afraid to argue for the sake of their families. She had read about the things the Third Reich did to their enemies, and to anyone else who disagreed with them.

She put her hand to her own throat, wondering if the same would happen to her as to the young soldier, and why it had not started yet.

'Are you alright?' Lance asked. His eyes searched her face and body. He looked as horrified as she felt, and she wondered if he were thinking the same about the young man.

'I think so,' she replied, unable to rise above a whisper. 'Yes. I am. I don't understand.'

'The poison sediment must have sunk to the bottom,' Lance suggested, but Nadine guessed that he did not believe it any more than she did.

'Drink the one on the left,' Devon commanded. Nadine was beginning to wonder who was in charge. Hardcastle had become the sidekick, though it was fair to say that he was looking rather ashen and a lot less sure of himself since the awful death of the soldier. 'You — ' Devon looked at her, but waved his gun at Lance. 'Drink it, now. All of it.'

'My left or your left?'

'I do not care, Miss Middleton. Just drain the cup.'

Nadine felt sure that her luck would not hold out for much longer. She had a fifty-fifty chance of being poisoned the moment the wine touched her lips.

'Hurry!' Devon snapped. 'Or Mr. Smith dies.'

She picked up the goblet, her hands shaking again. Her throat immediately contracted in protest at the danger. The first drop of fluid fell from her lips onto the floor. Like the other goblet, it tasted like ordinary sacramental wine. That did not stop Nadine from being sure she would be sick if she drank it all. Her stomach knotted so that the liquid felt trapped in her chest. Somehow, she managed to finish it. There was nothing at the bottom of the goblet.

'You!' Devon pointed to another soldier, clearly not prepared to risk his own safety. 'Take it from her and check.'

The young lad, who had just watched his friend die, did as he was bid. He looked into the goblet and shook his head. He even turned it upside-down, shaking it in case the key dropped out. Only a tiny drop of liquid that had pooled at the bottom fell onto the ground at his feet.

He shrugged, just as the ground around him suddenly gaped open into a pit and he fell in screaming.

Nadine instinctively reached for his hand, trying to save him, but the ground was determined to swallow him whole. He clung to her hand desperately, but his black leather gloves were slippery, and her hands were damp with perspiration. 'Lance, help me!' Nadine cried.

Lance caught the boy's other hand. Meanwhile, Hardcastle and Devon stood by and did nothing to save the soldier.

'Keep hold of my hand,' Lance said to the boy. 'I can't get a grip.'

They heard the click of a gun and looked up to see Devon had moved over to them. 'Let him go. He is nothing.'

'He's just a kid,' Lance said. His breath came in bursts from the exertion of trying to stop the boy from falling any further. 'They're all just stupid kids. Have some mercy, for God's sake, man.'

'I only believe in one god, and he knows that such boys are expendable! Let him go or I kill Miss Middleton.'

'Then shoot me,' said Nadine. 'Because I'm not letting go, and I think you need me to drink from that last goblet.' The boy was getting heavier and heavier, and neither Nadine nor Lance could hold him for much longer.

'Yes, you are right.' Devon pointed the gun at Lance.

'And if you shoot him, I'm never going to do it,' Nadine threatened.

'You are right again.' A shot rang out, and the young German soldier went limp. Devon had shot him in the head.

Nadine fell back in shock, letting go of the boy's hand at last. Lance also let go, and the boy fell into the pit. The ground immediately closed around him, and it was as if he had never been there.

'You monster.' Nadine sobbed quietly. Lance put his arm around her shoulders.

'The kid made his choice, honey,' he murmured to her. 'He chose his side and it took him straight to hell.'

'He was too young to understand,' she said. 'He'd been brainwashed. He was made to believe he was part of something important, yet the man who runs Germany cares nothing for his life.'

'You think your government cares any more for the lives of the young men it sends to war?' Devon raised a sarcastic eyebrow.

'I have to believe they do.'

'Just as we believe in what we are told,' Devon said.

'No.' Nadine shook her head. 'No, it's different. You have your master race and persecute those who don't fit in. We're not like that.'

Devon scoffed. 'Really? Hundreds of years ago, Jews were not allowed in Britain. What is the difference between Britain then and Germany now?'

'The people then were ignorant, and under the yoke of a church that told people what to think and feel,' Lance responded. 'We separated church and state to allow all men to live freely and without persecution.'

'This is a fine philosophical argument,' Hardcastle cut in. 'But it's not getting us that damn key. Devon, get on with it, will you? We're on a schedule here.'

'Drink from the last goblet,' Devon said to Nadine.

'I'll get drunk,' she said, but was surprised to find that was not true. The wine was not that strong. She wondered if it was mixed with water.

'I don't care,' said Devon, waving his gun around in a menacing fashion. 'Drink it now, please.'

Nadine had no alternative but to pick up the goblet. This time she did not hesitate. She had come to the conclusion that she was safe even if she drank the liquid. She did not understand why, but she did not question it either. She just thanked her lucky stars she was still alive.

When she drained the goblet, she looked inside and saw nothing. 'I don't understand . . . ' she said.

'Look underneath,' Lance told her.

She turned the goblet upside down and saw that the key was pressed into a recess on the bottom. It had been that simple all along, but she suspected the people who designed the test had been deliberately putting people off solving it.

'Take it out . . . slowly,' Hardcastle ordered. 'Then hand it to me.'

Nadine did as she was bid.

'And the other two keys?' Devon said. 'Quickly, or I shoot Mr. Smith.'

'You'll probably shoot him anyway,' Nadine said.

'You won't know until you hand me the other keys.'

She did not want to take the risk, so she took off her boot and turned it over, sliding open the secret compartment on the heel. She handed the two gold keys to Devon. Only then did she realise that she had nothing left to bargain with. Their lives would soon be over.

'And your father's journal?' Hardcastle said.

'I don't have it,' Nadine admitted. 'It was stolen from me.'

'Do not lie, Miss Middleton,' Devon warned.

'I'm not lying.'

'She's not lying,' said Lance. He reached into his back pocket and pulled out a dark brown journal. 'I've got it.'

'What?' Nadine turned to him. 'You stole it?'

'You were never going to give it to me, so I did what I had to do.'

'You betrayed me.' Her heart fell heavily in her chest. She had trusted him!

Lance shrugged. 'What are you going to do, honey?'

'Hand it over,' said Devon.

'No.' Lance shook his head. 'Do you think I'd be foolish enough to bring all the pages? I've buried some at an oasis not far from here. You take me with you, and I'll find them, and we go on together.'

'Lance?' Nadine still could not believe it. There must be some mistake. When he looked at her, his face was impassive, cold. There was no flicker of the emotions they had shared on their journey so far. Had it all been a lie?

'What do we do about her?' Hard-castle pointed to Nadine.

'Leave her here. She's never going to get out alive.'

'I could just shoot her,' said Devon.

'Then you lose me,' Lance said. He walked over to one of the candles and held the journal above it. 'I'm not interested in killing anyone, you under-stand? That's your bag. I'm only interested in knowledge. Take it or leave it. But if you shoot me now, the question is whether you can get to this journal before it burns up.' He let the candle catch the corner of the book, toying with it in the flames.

Nadine was literally speechless. Lance had been playing her all along.

Devon appeared to think about it for a brief moment, and then nodded. 'Very well. You come with us, and we leave the girl here.'

'You can't trust him, Lance,' Nadine was finally able to say.

'Don't think I don't know that,' Lance said. 'Any idea how we get out of here?' he asked Devon.

'We have left a trail back through the chamber and a rope down that long tunnel. Men are waiting to help us. Come. We don't have much time.'

'So long, honey,' Lance said to Nadine as they all left the church. 'I hope for your sake that these candles don't go out too soon.'

She could only watch them leave, with her father's journal and the three keys. She held it together until Lance closed the door after him, and then she put her head in her hands. He had betrayed her for the second time, but this time she would never forgive him.

12

Nadine knew she had little time for self-pity. She had to find a way out of the church before she died of starvation. She tried the door leading to the first chamber, but it had been locked and bolted from the other side.

As she walked past the candles, they all flickered as if a breeze had come from somewhere. What had Lance said? That he hoped they wouldn't all go out too soon? So what? It would be easy enough for her to relight the dead candles with the flames from those that stayed alight.

But what if they all went out? How did they manage to stay alight in the first place? Something had been said when they first arrived, but Nadine had seen so much horror since then that she could not remember exactly. She tried not to look at the German soldier who had burned to death, and tried not to think of the boy buried under the floor. Nevertheless, another chilly breeze made her shiver. The candles flickered again.

She spun around, wondering where the chill had come from. It had not come from the door leading to the first chamber. She was standing right next to that, and there was little or no air coming through it.

Walking slowly around the church, Nadine explored every nook and cranny. Oxygen came from somewhere, otherwise she would not be breathing. Not just oxygen, but a draught. She wondered what time it was on the outside. They had been underground for so long, it must be nearing night-time. As hot as Egypt was in the daytime, it became freezing cold when the sun went down.

She reached the altar, where it felt cooler still, and looked down at where the soldier had been buried. Could the breeze be coming from there? She hoped not, as she did not relish trying to find a way out past his body. She tried spilling more wine onto the ground, further away, in the hopes of opening up another recess, but to no avail.

'Probably just as well,' she murmured to herself. She had no guarantee that she would not be swallowed by the ground. That set her on another tangent. The one soldier had been swallowed by the earth. The other had been consumed by fire. 'Earth and fire . . . ' she whispered. 'Earth, wind and fire . . . ' Three elements!

The mantra her father had put in his journal came back to her. *Mix water with wine to reach the divine.*

She went to the baptismal font. There was water in that. Nadine looked back at the goblets. There would be very little wine, if any, left in them. One of the goblets was on the ground, where the soldier had fallen into the pit. If it were any of them, it would be the last one, which held the key. With no other option, Nadine picked up the last goblet and went to the font. She looked into the cup and saw that there were some dregs in the bottom. It was a long shot, but it was all she had. She used the cup to scoop up some water from the font, and drank the liquid down, whilst watching the font for something to happen. Nothing did happen there, but she heard a click behind her.

One of the statues above the altar — the one devoted to temperance — had opened up, and a rope ladder fell out of it.

'Yes!' she cried, dropping the goblet. She said in sardonic tones, 'Thanks for the help, Lance. I bet you didn't think of that when you mentioned the candles going out . . . ' She stopped. Had he thought of it? They had talked about who maintained the chambers when they arrived at the church. No, he could not have meant it as a way to help her get out. It was just a throwaway line meant to sap her confidence and let her know she was truly beaten. He had abandoned her, and she would definitely never forgive him.

For now, she had to get out and find a way to get to the last site before they did. An old cemetery, deep in the desert, was the last place in her father's journal. She was determined to stop the Germans getting the Eye of the Storm. She had seen at first hand how ruthless they could be, even to their own. With the power of the Eye, and the chance to see the future, who knew what havoc they might wreak?

Nadine went to the rope ladder and pulled herself up into a small aperture behind the statue. That led to an extremely narrow corridor, which she almost had to traverse sideways in order to get out. There was another rope ladder that appeared to lead to a wooden door in the ceiling. She climbed that and pulled herself out into the night. As she had thought, it was freezing cold, but that did not matter next to the fact that she was finally free.

Looking across the river, she saw that

she had come out on the other side.

She barely had time to celebrate before she heard a sound behind her. She turned and saw about a dozen or more people on horseback. Some held aloft torches, lit with paraffin. The first person she recognised was Mustafa.

'Are you planning to kidnap me again?' she asked.

'No. No kidnap!' He shook his head and laughed, and another man moved forward on a horse, followed by three other people. Nadine could just make out that they were two women and a man. The man who had moved forward first pulled the mask from his face and flashed the dazzling smile she knew so well.

'Prince Ari? But . . . you died.'

'I am glad to say that was not the truth.'

'What are you doing here? Are you going to kill me now?'

'Dear Miss Middleton, we are not here to kill you. We have been protecting you. Or, at least, we have been trying to. Please, let me introduce the Keepers of the Keys. It is our bounded duty to protect the keys from those who would use them for evil. I am Prince Ari, as you know. And these are . . . Miss Sutton and Mr. Barclay.'

Miss Sutton took off her veil, and the man called Mr. Barclay did the same. Only he was the one Nadine had known as the other woman's brother, Mr. Sutton.

'I'm so relieved you're not brother and sister!' Nadine blurted out. Miss Sutton looked a bit taken aback. She quickly glanced at the prince, so Nadine did not say anymore.

'Oh, and you know my wife, of course,' the prince said. 'Princess Valerie.'

Valerie took off her veil and smiled at Nadine. 'We've brought you a horse,' she said. 'I know you need an explanation, but first we must get you away to safety.'

'No, we have to get to the old cemetery,' said Nadine. 'They're on their way there.'

The prince spoke to Mustafa in Arabic, and then translated. 'Mustafa's scouts tell him that the Germans have stopped for the night to camp in the desert. They will not move on until daylight. Come, we must make our own camp. You must be hungry and tired after your labours.'

Nadine had no choice but to go with them, even though her head was reeling at the implications of the prince being alive. And the Keepers of the Keys? What was that all about? She had so many questions, but her companions refused to answer any of them until they had reached their destination.

Several hours later, deep into the night, they all sat around a campfire, next to an oasis very similar to the one where Mustafa had taken her the first time. For all Nadine knew, it was the very same one, but she did not really think so. They were much further south.

'You want explanations,' the prince

said. They had just eaten roast lamb and cool, refreshing yoghurt. Despite her longing for answers, and her heartache over Lance, Nadine found she had a huge appetite. The meal was followed with sweet black coffee that was the best she had ever tasted.

Valerie sat next to her husband, her head on his shoulder, but Nadine noticed that Miss Sutton and Mr. Barclay were on opposite sides of the fire, behaving very formally towards each other.

'Explanations would be good. Who died on the boat? Why did you not come forward and say it wasn't you? Why did Valerie just leave? Why did Mustafa kidnap me?'

The prince laughed and held up his hand. 'Please, we must start this story at the beginning, which is thousands of years ago. You know of the Eye of the Storm by now.'

'Yes.' Nadine nodded. 'It's a precious jewel which they say has the power to tell the future.'

'This is correct,' said the prince. 'No one knows when it first came into being or how, but for many centuries, even before your Christ walked the earth, it was believed that its powers were dangerous. The world then was not so big, so the jewel only had to be hidden from a few people. As the world grew, so did the fears for the stone. Not long after Christ died, a group — The Keepers of the Keys — was set up. Whilst much of the mythology used in hiding the jewel was Christian — '

'The four cardinal virtues,' Nadine interrupted.

'That is correct.' The prince nodded. 'Whilst the mythology is based on Christianity, we are not all Christians. I am a Muslim, Miss Sutton is Jewish, and Mr. Barclay is a Catholic priest.' That explained a lot about why Miss Sutton and Mr. Barclay hid their feelings, thought Nadine. The prince went on, 'There is a fourth keeper now, who replaced the last Keeper who died. He too is Christian-born, though I gather is he something of an agnostic.'

'Who is that?'

'Never mind. You cannot know all our secrets, Miss Middleton.' The prince smiled to show he meant no offence. 'There have always been four Keepers. Sometimes the duty is passed down from father to son. Sometimes from one person to another whom they believe is worthy. When we take on the role, we also take on a vow of celibacy.'

Nadine nodded, and looked from Miss Sutton to Mr. Barclay again. 'I see.'

'If we marry, then we must give up our role, though this is frowned upon and can lead to disgrace. I have been a Keeper since my father died when I was ten, and was supposed to renew my vows soon. I thought as a child that I could live that life. But then I met Valerie . . . ' He looked at his wife with love in his eyes. 'I knew immediately that I wanted to marry her, but my people forbade it. In marrying, I was letting down my heritage as Keeper. So

I faked my death to escape it, and Valerie left to join me.' The prince laughed. 'But that was not supposed to be how it happened. Valerie was to leave first.'

'With Mustafa . . . ' Nadine slapped her hand to her head.

'When you waved, Mustafa, who had never met Valerie, and only knew he was looking for a beautiful English rose, thought it was you. He took you, and he is very sorry about it.'

'Oh that's alright,' said Nadine. 'It was rather exciting really, and they were very kind to me. How is Akilah?'

Mustafa beamed when he heard his daughter's name, giving Nadine two thumbs-up.

'We could not have done it without her,' the prince said. 'She was able to find a body similar to mine — a young man who tragically died in a boating accident — and I was able to disappear. Only I still felt the weight of my desertion, and Valerie believed we owed it to you to still keep you safe.'

'Akilah is a clever girl.' Nadine smiled. 'So as Keepers of the Keys, you look after all the chambers where they're hidden?'

'That is correct.'

'So you know all the traps?'

The prince, Miss Sutton and Mr. Barclay shook their heads. 'No, we do not. A lot of the time we do not even know how they work. We know the safe ways in, but that is all.'

'So you know the safe way into the cemetery?'

'Yes, of course.'

'Good, because we have to go there. I don't have my father's journal anymore. Lance took it ... ' Nadine's voice faltered. 'I thought I could trust him, but ... '

'You mean this notebook?' Miss Sutton pulled a journal from the folds of her robes. 'Mr. Smith doesn't have it. I took it. I'm sorry, but we had to stall you somehow when we realised that Mr. Hardcastle and Mr. Devon were enemy spies.'

Nadine snatched it from her unceremoniously, and looked inside to see that it was indeed her father's journal.

'But Lance showed it to the Germans. He . . . lied to them.' Nadine put her hands to her face for the second time that day. 'He did tell me about the candles on purpose, so I would look for a way out. He saved my life. Oh God!' She jumped up. 'We have to go and save him. They'll kill him when they find out the truth!'

Nadine found a horse and clambered onto it, not caring that it did not have a saddle.

'Wait,' the prince called. 'You cannot go alone. You don't know where they are.'

'Then come with me and bring your men. I can't let him die. I love him.'

They were able to persuade her to wait half an hour until everyone was packed up and ready to leave. Valerie, Miss Sutton and Mr. Barclay said they would go on ahead to the cemetery and meet the others there.

'Mustafa will lead us to the Germans' camp,' the prince explained. 'Then we must find a way to free your Mr. Smith.'

'Thank you,' Nadine said. 'I know you don't have to help me.'

'We promised that we would protect you on your quest,' the prince said, mysteriously. He would not be drawn on the reason why. He only said, even more cryptically, 'Your coming was foretold.'

'By whom?'

'You will soon learn.'

They rode through the night, and stopped about a mile from the German encampment. There were a dozen or more tents, and also heavy artillery including jeeps and tanks. A fire burned in the centre of the camp and one figure sat there. 'Any further and they will see us,' said the prince. 'We must go the rest of the way on foot.'

They stole upon the camp silently, the sand crunching under their feet, but the Germans all seemed to be fast asleep in their tents. Only the one figure in front of the fire showed signs of movement. As they drew nearer still, Nadine's blood ran cold. It was the old Arab she had seen several times in the distance. He must have been working for the Germans all along.

'They're not here,' he said in an English accent as they moved in behind him. 'The camp is a dummy to put you off the scent. They're already on their way to the cemetery.'

He turned around, and Nadine thought for a moment that she had seen a ghost. An icy finger touched her spine, and she closed her eyes — then opened them again, sure she must be dreaming. Only it was not a dream.

'Hello, princess,' he said.

'Dad?'

258

13

'I knew you wouldn't be able to resist following the clues,' Raleigh Middleton said to his daughter as they rode towards the cemetery.

For many miles they had ridden fast, with Nadine taking the lead, eager to get to Lance; but the horses were tired, and had slowed to a steady trot.

'Are you one of the Keepers of the Keys?' Nadine asked.

'Yes, princess. I took on the role when the last Keeper died a few months ago. Can you guess who that was?'

'No . . . I mean . . . ' Things were starting to become clear to Nadine. 'You mean *Mum*? But how could she be a Keeper of the Keys? She married and had a child. It's not allowed.'

'Yes, and her people were not pleased, until I was able to work out that it was meant to be. Your coming was foretold, Nadine.'

She looked at her father, and for the first time ever saw a sort of madness in his eyes. 'You're the Chosen One,' he continued.

Nadine scoffed. 'No, I'm not. I'm just a normal girl.'

'That's what your mother always said. That's why she took you away from me. She said I wasn't safe around you. She said lots of other things too, about how I'd only married her to find the Eye of the Storm.'

'And did you?' Nadine asked, flatly.

He faltered a little before insisting, 'Of course not. I loved your mother. There was a time when she trusted me.'

'Not enough to tell you the quick way into the chambers,' Nadine pointed out.

'You didn't have to go in the quick way. You had to overcome all the tests, Nadine, and you did it. Just as it was foretold. I couldn't have done it, even by taking the shortcuts. It is a sad fact that the Keepers of the Keys are denied the right to use them.'

Nadine stopped her horse. 'Let me get one thing straight. I am only going to the cemetery to save the man I love. Once I've found him, I'm leaving with him; and as far as I'm concerned, that bloody stone can stay hidden for another two thousand years!'

'Nadine, princess . . . '

'Don't, Dad! Don't call me princess. You put my life in danger just so you could see what the Eye does, didn't you?' All her life she had hero-worshipped her father, but the man before her was weak, and not a little bit mad. Her mother must have felt betrayed when she realised that the man she loved had only married her to get closer to the stone. Yet she had never criticised him to Nadine. Never stopped her from seeing him.

'I'm a scientist. It's my job to seek out the truth.'

'No, I don't think that's it. I think you want the Eye for yourself, and you were willing to lose Mum and risk my life in order to get it. Did you tell Lance to write those things in the scientific journal?'

'Yes.'

'But not to protect the Eye.'

'I needed to give you a purpose, so that you would fight to clear my name — and you rose to the challenge, just as I always thought you would.'

'But you knew I loved him, Dad. I told you.'

Her father's lips pursed irritably. 'Love is not important, Nadine. You have a greater purpose.'

'I am not your Chosen One. I am your daughter, yet that seems to mean nothing to you!'

She galloped off into the distance, joining the prince and Mustafa at the head of the group.

'Miss Middleton?' The prince looked at her askance.

It was one of the hardest things she had ever had to say. 'You can't trust him. My father, I mean. He can't be trusted. Whatever he's convinced you of, he's either wrong or lying or both. Tell me, how are Keepers chosen?'

'It is foretold.'

'By whom?'

'We don't know. We only know that those chosen share a bloodline going way back in time.'

'So you share a bloodline with my mother, which makes us sort of — what? Cousins?'

'Yes, we are sort of cousins.'

'Well, I'm glad of that anyway, cousin.' Nadine smiled and he returned the favour, bowing his head in acceptance. 'But my father doesn't share the bloodline, so how did he become a Keeper?'

'He shares your bloodline, and you are . . .'

'Oh, don't say I'm the Chosen One, Prince Ari, please. Whatever he's said, he's fooled you into letting him have a part in all this. I'm sorry. I really am. Why would it be me, rather than you? You're Egyptian. This is your country.

Why would a white woman from Britain be the chosen one? My father has just pulled everyone into his self-aggrandizing scheme. This is not about me, or anyone else. It's about him finding the stone and claiming the credit for it, even if he has to do it vicariously through me.'

'From what I have seen, even if your father has lied to us about his role in all of this, he has not lied about yours. You have passed every test so far. No one has ever done that.'

'A lot of it is just common sense, Prince Ari. That's all.'

'Did common sense save you from being burnt to death or swallowed up into a pit by drinking the wine?'

'Oh, I don't know. Lance said there are things we don't always know; things that we think are magic when really there's a rational explanation. I'd rather believe him. I'm really not comfortable with this 'Chosen One' rubbish. I respect everyone's right to believe what they want, but I don't want to be anyone's messiah. It never ends well, and I don't much fancy being crucified.'

'I will not let that happen.' He spoke with deep sincerity.

'Valerie is a very lucky girl,' Nadine said. 'If you weren't married to her, and I wasn't so stupidly in love with Lance, I'd marry you myself.'

'Now you tell me!' The prince laughed. 'But really, I am content with the woman I have chosen.'

'Then she's a much luckier chosen one than I am.'

'I am the lucky one,' the prince said.

'Yes, I'll agree with that!'

It was early evening when they finally reached the cemetery. They took up camp behind a sand dune and watched through binoculars as the Germans went about their business in the graveyard. They appeared to be digging willy-nilly, with no real idea where to find the last key.

Nadine's heart leapt when she saw Lance amongst them. He was hand-cuffed and clearly a prisoner, but he was alive. She guessed that he had somehow managed to stall them on the matter of the journal and the extra pages. That did not explain how he had known to bring them to the cemetery.

'Do you remember the riddle?' Raleigh Middleton asked Nadine.

'No,' she lied.

'Please, darling. Don't be angry with me. I know you've memorised everything.'

'Haven't you?' she asked.

'It's been a while since I've seen the book. I know that courage or fortitude is the last virtue.'

'It's, *'You'll need the courage of a lion when you find this broken column.'* The lion and the broken column are two of the symbols used to signify courage.'

'Clever girl.' Raleigh went to pat Nadine's arm, but she moved away from him.

She wanted to get a closer look at Lance, to make sure they had not harmed him. As she moved to the top of the sand dune, her foot slipped, and she went sliding down the bank, leaving her in sight of the Germans.

'No,' she hissed quickly, as she saw the prince and Mustafa attempt to come to grab her back. 'Wait there.'

Several soldiers ran up to her, and caught her by the arms, marching her down into the cemetery.

Mr. Hardcastle and Mr. Devon were overseeing the digging-up of one of the graves. They stopped what they were doing and walked across to Nadine.

'What brings you here, Miss Middleton?' Hardcastle asked. He was quite friendly, considering the circumstances.

'I've come to stop you,' she said, with more courage than she actually felt.

Both men laughed. Lance smiled, but he did not seem to be mocking her.

'You have been led here under false pretences,' she told them. 'My father is . . . was . . . a madman. There is no Eye of the Storm. Or if there is, it is merely a jewel like any other.'

'You forget, Miss Middleton,' said

Devon, 'that we saw what happened in the church yesterday. One man burst into flames and another was swallowed by a pit. Yet you survived it all. Which makes me wonder . . . perhaps your being here is fortuitous. Mr. Smith here, who seems to have lost the papers he hid, has given us some clue about 'Being brave will find the right grave'. Is that correct?'

Lance's eyes glinted in the sunlight. Nadine had trouble keeping a straight face. 'It sounds about right to me.'

'So maybe,' said Devon, 'if I point this gun at your head, it will help you to find the right grave.'

'Or you could just shoot me and you'd never find it.'

'Shall I shoot Mr. Smith instead? You have already shown how attached to him you are. It is a strange way to feel about a man who betrayed you only yesterday.'

'I'm not here for him. I'm here to get the Eye for myself. You can't be trusted with it, and neither can he. So shoot him if you have to.' Nadine hoped that her voice did not tremble too much. She could not let them know how much Lance really meant to her. 'Once he's dead, you'll have nothing left to bargain with. But I should warn you that I'm the Chosen One, apparently, so if you kill me or upset me, I can make sure you'll never find it.'

Lance's head snapped up and he had a wary look in his eyes. He imperceptibly shook his head, but Nadine had gone too far to back down now. She was playing for both their lives and the more convincing she sounded the better, even if she did not believe herself to be the so-called Chosen One.

Something changed in Devon's eyes. It was a hint of recognition. 'The Chosen One? What do you know of this?'

'Not much, only that it's me. My mother was a Keeper of the Key, and my coming was foretold. You know how it goes. Into every generation a something or other is born who will do something or other. Noah, Moses, Nadine Middleton. You can see the connection, I'm sure. I hope you've got a boat. Water always seems to play a part, either flooding everything or parting just when it needs to, so it could get a bit wet; and we are in Egypt, after all.'

'If you're the Chosen One, what do you know of this graveyard?' asked Hardcastle. He seemed to be veering between disbelieving and accepting everything she said at face value.

'It's a cemetery,' Nadine said.

'That much we know,' said Devon.

'It was excavated in the late nineteen-twenties. That was something of a rescue project, due to the dam they're building at Aswan. No one knows who the people in the cemetery are, but they're thought to be from the court of Nobatia. They also found a crown here from pre-Christian times.' Nadine's father had told them all this before they arrived at the cemetery.

'What is the next riddle?' asked

Devon. 'The real riddle, Miss Middleton.'

'*You'll need the courage of a lion when you find this broken column,*' Nadine said, truthfully. She did not have time to think of anything different. 'The lion and the broken column are symbols linked to the cardinal virtue: courage. Your poor dead men had more of that than you, so I presume you'll let a few more die before taking a risk yourself.'

Devon replied by slapping Nadine hard across the face. Lance instinctively surged forward, swearing and threatening to kill Devon, but his hands were bound and a group of the soldiers held him back.

'Find something with a lion or a broken column,' Devon barked at his men. He spoke again in German and Nadine guessed he was giving the same order. 'You!' He pointed at Nadine. 'You will also look. But don't try anything, or I will shoot Mr. Smith just for the hell of it. He has been driving me crazy with his American jokes.'

'That sounds just like him,' Nadine agreed.

The graves in the cemetery were under artificial mounds. The soldiers had been digging into most of them, uncovering large monoliths. Several of them were broken, and so could easily have fit what Nadine was looking for. But nothing stood out to her as the right one.

She made several rounds of the cemetery, but having Devon and Hardcastle on her heels, plus the threat of death to Lance, did not much help her concentration. She was also torn as to what to do. If she found the right column, did she tell them? Or did she pretend she had found it when she had not? Then she would have to work out how she could escape with Lance before the Germans found out she had lied to them.

It gave her hope to know that the prince and Mustafa were waiting with their men in the dunes. But, as an army, they were outmatched by the Nazis. Their guns were older and they didn't have as many. She did not have Devon's blasé attitude to men dying. Every life, to Nadine, was an important life.

'Have they hurt you?' she asked Lance quietly when Hardcastle and Devon were occupied elsewhere. He had a bruise across his cheekbone.

'Not too much. I'm alright, Nadine. You have to stop thinking about me and get yourself out of here.'

'Why? Because I'm the Chosen One?' she scoffed.

'No. Because I'm desperately in love with you, and I don't want them to hurt you after I'm dead.'

'Don't say that!' Nadine stopped and turned to him. 'I also . . . ' She almost blurted out the truth about her father, but did not want to alert Devon and Hardcastle to the spectators in the dunes. 'I understand more, now so I don't blame you anymore for what you did. We were both deceived.'

Lance squinted in the late-afternoon

sun, as if trying to decipher the code she was attempting to convey.

'Please,' said Devon. 'This is most touching, but we have work to do.' He clicked his pistol and pointed it directly at Lance's temple. 'Find the way in to get the last key, or I will shoot him.'

'It's over there.' Nadine pointed back the way they came. 'I found it ten minutes ago, but thought that Mr. Hardcastle needed the exercise.'

'Cheeky — ' Hardcastle muttered an expletive.

'Don't play games, Miss Middleton.' Devon pushed the pistol against Lance's skin. 'I will kill him.'

'Then I won't help you. You don't have the key yet.'

'As soon as I do, you will be dead, young lady.'

That was what Nadine had thought; so, the more she played for time, the better. She did not want to make either Lance or herself expendable.

'But you don't know what the fifth virtue is,' Nadine said.

'What?' Devon pulled the gun away from Lance's head. 'What sort of game is this? I only know of four virtues.'

'No, there were five. Actually, there are seven in all, but the fifth virtue is all about what happens when you find the Eye. If you don't know what it is, you cannot use the Eye. It's in the rules.'

'You're lying.'

'No, I'm not. In my father's journal the last page held the words '*The Fifth Virtue*', with a question mark. He did not know what it was. But I do. I've worked it out.'

'She's making it up as she goes along,' said Hardcastle. It was closer to the truth than Nadine cared to admit.

Nadine reached into the voluminous pocket in her waistcoat and pulled out her father's journal to gasps from Devon and Hardcastle.

'You had it all along. He lied to us!'

'Of course he lied to you. But I'm not.' She had taken the journal back from Miss Sutton before they parted.

Not even her father knew that she had it. 'Look . . . '

Nadine opened the journal to the last page. It was blank except for the words *The Fifth Virtue?* It was just as she had said. 'My father died before he could find out the truth.'

'There are seven virtues in the Catholic catechism,' Hardcastle said, turning to Devon and speaking as if they were the only two there. 'Prudence, Justice, Temperance, Fortitude, Faith, Hope and Charity. So, it's one of the other three. Faith, Hope or Charity.'

'With all the religious connotations of this quest, it must be faith,' said Devon. 'I have faith in my Fuhrer, so it is enough for me. What do you believe in, Hardcastle?'

'I don't have much faith in him,' Hardcastle said. 'I might admire his ideas, but I'm only in this for the money, remember?'

'So if it is not faith, but hope, then the Third Reich hopes for a better world,' Devon mused. 'Or charity? What

276

would charity mean?'

'Giving the stone away?' Hardcastle suggested.

'No, that will not happen. It is charity to one's fellow man.'

Nadine snorted with laughter. 'I hardly think the Third Reich can claim that, with the way they're persecuting the innocent. You were not exactly charitable to those boys who died, either.'

'We will work it out when we get there,' Devon said, pointedly ignoring her. 'If I have to torture it out of her, I will. Let us get through this phase first and find the last key. Now . . . ' He turned to Nadine. 'Your boyfriend's time is running out, so show us the way to find the key.'

Nadine took them back to one of the mounds. That had a broken pillar inside it, but on the pillar was the outline of a plant. It was rather primitive, but Nadine had immediately recognised it as a palm leaf, which was one of the symbols of courage and fortitude.

'I do not see,' said Devon.

'In the Gospels,' Nadine explained, as patiently as if speaking to children, 'Jesus rode into Jerusalem on Palm Sunday. The day before he had looked at the great city and wept, because he knew what awaited him there. Yet he still went, showing great courage in the face of his death. It's a fitting symbol of courage.'

'What do these Egyptians know about Christianity?' asked Hardcastle. 'They're all Muslims, aren't they?'

'The religion doesn't matter,' Nadine said. 'The quest has drawn from all sorts of different belief systems. It's the symbolism that matters.'

'But,' Lance cut in, 'this area had quite a large Christian settlement at one point, so it's not unheard of to find this symbolism here. Egypt has a vast history, encompassing many beliefs. It's not surprising they overlap here as they do in many countries. What is Easter Sunday but an attempt by the Church to take over what was formerly a pagan ritual and put their own stamp on it?'

'So,' said Devon, sounding bored with the theological discussion, 'what do we do with this symbol? Do you say a prayer over it, Miss Middleton?' His tone was mocking.

'If you don't believe, you're not going to find it,' Nadine chided. She stepped forward and put her hand on the palm leaf. It was never that easy . . . but worth a try. As she did, the broken pillar swayed. She reached into the sand around it, and pulled it towards her. 'Help me,' she said.

Devon barked orders at his soldiers, clearly not wanting to risk his own neck to move it. They helped Nadine pull down the pillar. The bank of sand moved aside, to show a dark entrance into what appeared to be another staircase.

'Bring torches and rope,' Devon ordered his men. 'Someone stay up here and hold the rope. Make sure this entrance does not close! We do not want to get trapped down there.'

They followed the steps downwards into a dimly-lit cavern. 'I wish they'd varied their decorating skills a little,' Nadine quipped to Lance.

'Yep. Seen one dark chamber at the end of a long drop, you've seen them all. It's been fun, though, hasn't it?'

Nadine paused. 'Yes, yes it's been great fun. Whatever else happens, Lance, I'm so glad you're here with me.'

'Yeah, me too, babe.'

Tears pricked her eyes. They might not have much longer left if she could not stall the Germans with the fifth virtue. 'I'm sorry I doubted you.'

Lance looked at her long and hard. 'I guess you know the truth now, huh?'

'Yes . . . Did you know all of it?'

'No. No, I didn't know all of it. I swear.'

'What are you two babbling on about?' asked Hardcastle. They were nearing the end of the staircase.

'None of your damn business,' Lance said.

'A man and his wife are entitled to privacy,' Nadine said.

'Was that a yes?' asked Lance. 'Finally?'

'I suppose it was.' She blushed.

'You'll look very pretty, buried together,' said Devon, rushing past them down the last few steps. Several soldiers followed him.

He stopped suddenly, as they all did, when there came a low growl from the dimly-lit chamber.

14

A pair of shining eyes came out of the darkness. Devon backed up the stairs, almost falling over Lance and Nadine as he did so.

'It's a real lion,' Nadine said, as the animal came into the light of the torches. 'Was it too much to hope it was metaphorical? Really?'

'At least it's not another dark pit,' Lance offered.

'True; they were getting a bit monotonous.'

The lion was magnificent, with a brown and black mane. He growled and set down low on his haunches, ready to pounce. The question was: where would he go first? Lance and Nadine were further up the steps. Devon and the soldiers were between them and the lion.

'Looks hungry, too,' said Lance.

Devon raised his pistol and pointed it at the animal. He pulled back the hammer . . .

'No!' Nadine rushed at Devon and the shot from the pistol went wide, sparing the animal. 'Don't shoot him. He can't help being trapped down here. He didn't ask for this life. Anyway, what's courageous about shooting an animal that can't shoot back? Any fool can do that! Do you want to find this key or not?'

'Of course I want to find the key, and that animal is in my way,' Devon said. He reloaded his gun. 'So he will die.'

'No, he won't,' Nadine said emphatically. 'That's not the way this works. Haven't you worked that out that yet? There are no easy ways through the tests. The whole point is that you have to earn the keys. If you shoot the lion, something will happen that will kill us all. I know it.'

Devon's eyes flickered with doubt, but he stayed his hand and put the gun back in its holster.

The animal seemed to be waiting. Or perhaps he was choosing which of them he would have for supper. Whilst they were on the staircase, the lion stayed below. She wondered if he had been trained to do that.

'So, Miss Middleton,' Hardcastle said after a few minutes had passed, 'how do we get past the lion?'

'I haven't worked that out yet,' she said. 'I am making this up as I go along, you know.' That was truer than she dared to admit, but she hoped she could keep them fooled for a little while longer. At least, until she found a way for her and Lance to escape their clutches or for the prince to bring reinforcements. With any luck he had already made his way to the easy route out of the chamber.

Devon sighed impatiently and tried to take a step down the staircase. As he did, the lion growled and moved forward a few inches, causing the man to jump back a step.

'You go,' he said to Nadine. 'Go and

get past the lion, now or I shoot your boyfriend.'

'You're very fond of threats, aren't you?' said Nadine. 'Doesn't it occur to you that being shot and killed quickly is preferable to being savagely mauled by a lion?'

'Yeah, thanks honey,' said Lance, wryly.

Devon ignored Nadine and pointed the gun at Lance's head again. 'Go,' he said to her.

Nadine took a deep breath and went down the staircase a few steps. The lion continued with a low growl, but did not move. 'Nice lion,' she said. 'You wouldn't want to eat me. I'm too skinny. Wait for Mr. Hardcastle. He's got plenty of meat on him.'

'Oi!'

Nadine had reached the bottom step, sure that at any moment the lion would pounce and maul her. Her legs trembled violently as she took the last step. Still the lion continued to growl, but did not move. 'Good boy,' she whispered. 'Good boy.'

She went around him, inching into the darkness of the chamber. 'I can't see,' she said. Devon threw her a battery torch, which she switched on.

'Find the key,' he ordered. 'Quickly.'

'I am going as quickly as I dare, Mr. Devon,' she protested. 'If you would like to try walking around this very dangerous lion yourself to get things done quicker, do be my guest.'

'It seems that he likes you more than he likes me,' Devon pointed out.

'I wonder why. Perhaps it's because I didn't immediately point a gun at him.'

Nadine shone the torch over the walls, all the time aware of the lion waiting in the centre. As she turned, so did he, watching her every move. She was more vaguely aware of Devon giving a quiet command to one of the soldiers, who moved down the steps, behind the lion's back.

'I don't think . . . ' she began to say, when the lion turned quickly and pounced on the soldier, giving out a mighty roar. The boy screamed, and was thrown back into the darkness. For a few minutes there was the dreadful sound of the lion's teeth chomping, then silence.

Nadine turned on Devon, tears of anger streaming down her cheeks. 'You really don't care who gets hurt, do you? You make me sick!'

'Find the key,' Devon said through gritted teeth, but he was clearly shaken by events. He had moved to the lowest step. 'Hurry, or . . .'

'Or what? You'll kill Lance?' Nadine snorted with laughter. 'So you keep saying.' She turned to the lion. 'Come here, boy. Come along.'

The lion tamely came to her side, and — after a moment's hesitation, because of the terrible thing the animal had just done — Nadine put her hands in his mane and stroked him, noticing that he wore a collar of some kind.

The soldier's death was not his fault. He had only done what he was born to do. 'You are a good boy, aren't you?

And I think you're trained to do whatever I want. So, if I wanted to set you on Mr. Devon . . . '

'What are you doing?' Devon said, his jaw tightening.

'I think, Mr. Devon, you're going to undo Lance's handcuffs and let him come to me. If you don't, then I'll set this lion on you.' Nadine had no idea if she had the courage to do that, but she wanted him to believe that she could if she wanted to.

Devon's face went through a myriad of emotions. Humour, doubt, anger, more doubt. Then he raised his gun and shot the lion.

'No!' Nadine screamed as the animal slumped at her feet. She crouched down and stroked him. 'I'm so sorry,' she said. With her back to Devon, she quickly took off the lion's collar and shoved it into her pocket.

'Now,' said Devon, coming down off the last step, and coming further into the chamber. 'Find the key.'

'You're a monster,' Nadine said,

crying genuine tears of remorse for the animal.

But Devon was not listening. He had turned suddenly and was looking at something in the shadows on the far side of the chamber. 'No,' he whispered. He tried to make it back to the steps, but he was too late. Another lion, a female this time, who had been waiting in the darkness for her moment — or, thought Nadine, had been let into the chamber by someone — pounced and killed Devon instantly.

Nadine shut her eyes and only opened them when she felt a warm nose against her hand. It was the female. 'I'm sorry,' Nadine said to her. 'I truly am. It isn't fair that they made him do this.' She gestured to the male lion. 'Or you.' Her heart filled with anger, and she stood up and glared at everyone still standing on the stairs.

'This is ridiculous,' she said, her eyes flaming. Somehow she was angrier about the dead lion than any of the other lives lost during the quest.

Perhaps because human beings chose the stupid things they did, whereas animals only acted on instinct. 'Innocent people and these beautiful animals have been manipulated for centuries, and all to find some stone. What sort of sick human being came up with all these tests that steal young lives and stop people who love each other from being together? Where is the virtue in killing people? Where is the glory in that? What does all this prove? Nothing! Nothing!'

'Well, thank God Devon has gone,' said Hardcastle, ignoring Nadine's tirade. He was not foolish enough to come down the stairs. 'He was getting far too big for his jackboots. Now I'm in charge again. Give me the key, Miss Middleton. Oh, and you might reach into Devon's pocket and get the other three,' he added to the SS men.

'I don't know where it is,' said Nadine.

'I know that you do. Look, I'll let Mr. Smith go.' Hardcastle threw a set of keys towards Lance. 'Believe it or not, I'm not mad on all this killing. It's not what I signed up for. I just want the stone. Now, be a good girl and give me the key.' The soldiers looked uncertain, but with Devon dead, they were unsure who to follow.

As Lance joined her, Nadine took the key out of her pocket and threw it to Hardcastle. 'Go on, go and leave us be.'

'Thank you,' Hardcastle said. 'So now where do I go?'

Nadine gave him a set of coordinates which she had seen on the penultimate page of her father's journal. 'I've no idea where that is. It could be in Egypt. It could be in Cheltenham for all I know.'

He stood for a moment looking at her. 'You're a remarkable young woman, Miss Middleton.'

'Oh, yes, I'm the Chosen One. Aren't I lucky that so many people died so I can complete this quest? Somehow I don't feel very proud of myself, Mr. Hardcastle. If you've any sense, you'll throw that stone away when you get it. Or don't go for it at all. There'll only be more death. Maybe even yours.'

'I'll take my chances,' Hardcastle said. He turned and ordered the soldiers to leave, following them back up the stairs. Nadine felt sure something would happen to prevent the men's escape, but nothing did. Whatever traps the chamber held were probably only down with the lions. Sometimes it only took something very simple to test a person's courage.

'One more thing,' Hardcastle called, when he reached the top of the staircase. 'What's this fifth virtue that I need to know about?'

'That's something you have to work out for yourself to be worthy,' Nadine said.

'Right . . . ' Hardcastle sounded doubtful, but with the four keys and the coordinates to the site of the jewel, he no longer cared.

'Please tell me you didn't give him the real key,' Lance said when they were sure Hardcastle had gone. He put his arms around Nadine. She fell against him, exhausted with emotion.

'What makes you think I switched it?'

'Well, if you can scrawl 'The Fifth Virtue?' into your father's journal to gain more time, I'm pretty sure you could arrange with the prince to bring a dummy key.'

'How do you know what was in my father's journal?'

'He let me read it, several times, and I know for a fact there was nothing scrawled on the last page. Besides, it wasn't his writing. Hardcastle is right, my love. You are a remarkable woman.' He kissed her to the sound of low growling. 'Now, can you lead me out of this lions' den? I don't think they like me as much as they like you.'

As they left, the female lion lay down by her mate and licked his face. Three cubs came out of the shadows and nestled against their mother.

★ ★ ★

'Is it all my fault they're all dead?' Nadine whispered to Lance several hours later. It was dark and they lay in a tent, alone together. The group, including the prince, Mustafa and Raleigh Middleton had made camp at another oasis, some miles from where the stone was said to be hidden. Neither Lance nor Nadine had said much to her father, united in their disappointment at being manipulated and lied to.

'Why would you think that?' he asked.

'Because they all followed me. Because I somehow had the answers and they didn't.'

Lance turned to face her, cradling her in one arm, whilst stroking her hair with his free hand. Flickering lanterns illuminated the tent, casting their shadows on the walls. 'They made their choice, Nadine. They chose to work for the forces of darkness.'

'Who gets to decide that, Lance? Who knows which is the right side and which is the wrong side?'

'You think Hitler is right about everything?'

'No, of course not. But those boys . . . they were ordered to come here. Even Devon was ordered to come here.'

'They could have refused or deserted, darling. They didn't.'

Nadine was not so sure about that.

'Even if the German kids couldn't argue with their leader, Devon could have,' Lance continued. 'Hardcastle still could. He's not German. He's British, but he has turned his back on his own country, and for less reason than Devon. For Devon, it at least seemed ideological, even if we don't agree with him. Hardcastle has done it for cold, hard cash. He wants to be on the winning side, because the winning side will buy more weapons.'

'Do you think he'll die? In this final quest? I don't want another death on my conscience, Lance. Not even that of a traitor.'

'Like I said, people make their own choices about where they want to be.

You can't stop them or prevent the consequences.'

'What about you? What if you get killed? So far we've been really lucky, but I can't help thinking that this next quest will be dangerous for us all.'

'The others haven't exactly been a walk in the park.'

'I know, but if this jewel does what they say it does, that's a lot of power. I don't think any of us are supposed to have that power.'

'So let's not go,' Lance suggested. 'Hardcastle doesn't have the last key. We could run away from here. Get as far away as possible. Throw the key in the deepest part of the ocean if we have to, so that no one ever gets it.'

'Yes!' Nadine sat up, pulling the blanket around her bare chest. 'Of course we could. Perhaps that's what I'm supposed to do.' It seemed as if a weight had been lifted from her shoulders, and with such a simple solution. 'When can we leave?'

'With you looking like that, I'd kinda

like to wait until morning. We'll wake before anyone else and take off.'

'Do you really mean it, Lance?' Nadine looked down at him and stroked his face. 'Won't you be a bit sorry you never found out the truth?'

'I didn't come to Egypt for the stone, Nadine. I came here for you. I told you that, but you didn't believe me. Well, believe me now. All I ever wanted was to take care of you.'

She bent down and kissed his mouth. The kiss became deeper and more passionate. She eased herself across so that she was on top of him. 'Why haven't we been doing this all the time?' she teased. 'It's more fun than digging up old relics.'

Lance flipped her over so that their positions were altered. 'Wait till you find out what other tricks I've got up my sleeve.'

'Why, Professor Smith, I'm shocked.'

'Are you?' He looked worried for a moment, until Nadine giggled.

'And delighted,' she added quickly,

pulling him down to her.

* * *

They finally fell fast asleep in the early hours, waking much later than they intended. They dressed hurriedly.

'Where is it?' Nadine asked. 'Lance, have you taken it?' She looked at him accusingly.

'Taken what?'

'The key. It was in my boot, but it's gone.'

'I haven't got it, Nadine, I swear. Check again, in case you've missed it.'

'There aren't many places to miss it in the heel of my boot.' Nadine went out of the tent and looked around. Prince Ari and Mustafa were sitting by the fire, drinking coffee. They waved to her and bid her to come over.

'Have you seen my father?' she asked them.

'He was up earlier this morning, but I think he went back to bed,' the prince replied.

Nadine went to her father's tent, but it was completely empty. He had gone — and she knew without question that he had taken the key with him.

15

They rode south for most of the morning, changing horses at another oasis, before setting off again. This time they rode deep into the desert. The Nile still flowed beside them, but there was very little in the way of civilisation. Somewhere along the way, Miss Sutton, Mr. Barclay and Valerie joined them.

'Mustafa says there is a sandstorm coming in,' the prince told them as they neared their destination. 'We must hurry and take cover.'

They found the site of an ancient town, with over a dozen pyramids of varying sizes. Due to the severe location, they had not kept as well as those at Giza. Many were corroded: some no more than stones sticking out of the sand. But some of the smaller pyramids appeared to be in almost new condition.

The group stayed back out of sight, partially hidden by a sand dune.

The Germans were already there, digging in a haphazard way around the largest pyramid. Hardcastle sat atop a smaller pyramid, shouting orders. Someone sat a few feet below him, also watching the activity.

'It's my dad,' Nadine said to Lance. He nodded. There was little else to say.

Mustafa said something in Arabic, and the prince translated. 'It is said that Moses came to this place. He released birds that ate the serpents owned by the enemy.'

'I don't suppose we have any of those,' Nadine said. 'Or a plan of any kind?'

'You should speak to your father,' the prince suggested. 'Appeal to his better self.'

'I'm afraid I don't think he has one,' she replied. 'All my life I looked up to him, but he's just a graverobber when all is said and done.' She sighed. 'There's only one way to do this.' She looked at Lance. 'Do you want to get captured with me? Or are you going to wait here and rescue me when things get bad?'

'When you put it like that . . . ' Lance said. 'I'm coming with you. The prince and Mustafa here can rescue us.'

'Remember, Miss Middleton,' the prince warned, 'you have nothing left to barter with.'

'I have the Fifth Virtue.'

'Which doesn't exist,' Lance reminded her.

'Well, I say it does, and I'm the Chosen One. Apparently.'

'When you tell them that,' Lance suggested, 'leave out the 'apparently'. If you don't believe it, they won't.'

'Stay here,' Nadine said to the prince and the others. 'Don't get involved unless you have to. I don't want to be responsible for anyone else's death.'

'Miss Middleton,' said the prince. 'You forget that we have chosen to be here, to help you with your quest.'

'A few days ago, you faked your

death so that you could get married. You're only here because Valerie shamed you into it. No — ' Nadine put up her hand to stop the prince from speaking. 'None of that was meant to be a criticism. I applaud what you did. This stone has caused too much suffering. Well if I am the Chosen One, I say you should all go away and be safe and happy. You with Valerie, Miss Sutton with Mr. Barclay. No one should have to miss out on love and happiness because of this. Otherwise, what exactly are we protecting here?'

'You are a remarkable woman, Miss Middleton,' the prince said.

'So everyone keeps telling me. I'm not though. I'm just a secretary from London and not a very good one at that. You're the remarkable ones, living with this burden all your lives. I've only had to put up with it a few days.'

Nadine and Lance rode out into the open; quietly to begin with, so as not to alert the Germans and Hardcastle to their presence in case it also gave up the location of the prince and the others.

'We wondered how long it would take you to arrive,' said Hardcastle from atop the pyramid as soon as they were in sight. The pyramid was only about twenty feet high. 'Didn't we, Raleigh?'

'I knew you'd come,' Nadine's father said. 'That's why I took the key.'

They both started to climb down.

'Yes, I know,' she said to her father. 'You manipulated me, just as you have done all along.'

'It's all for the best, princess.'

'Don't call me 'princess', Dad. You've lost the right to do that. You used me and Mum to this end. Well I hope it will make you happy. Because you won't have a family. You won't have a daughter.'

Her father's eyes showed genuine pain. 'Nadine . . . '

'You're the only one who can get into this thing,' Hardcastle said. 'I was angry when I found you'd given me the wrong key, but I understand better now. We were never going to get anywhere without you. And it turns out that Raleigh and I want the same thing. We want to see that stone. We want to know what it does. It doesn't matter that we're working for different purposes.'

'If I get it for you, will you promise to leave us be?' Nadine asked.

'Of course. I already told you, I'm not into all this killing. I just want results. So, Miss Middleton ... ' Hardcastle reached the bottom of the pyramid, somewhat out of breath. 'Where do we find it? Something to do with this fifth virtue, eh?'

Nadine almost told him the truth, about there being no fifth virtue, and she wondered why her father had not. It was all she had to play with, so the longer Hardcastle believed it, the better.

'Perhaps,' she said. 'Give me the keys.'

Hardcastle was reluctant at first, but he handed them over. Nadine started to walk around the camp, looking at each pyramid in turn. Lance, Hardcastle and her father followed her. Meanwhile, the German soldiers continued to work on the largest pyramid.

'You're looking in the wrong place,' she said.

'Why? The jewel would belong to the richest person, wouldn't it?' Hardcastle asked.

'Not necessarily. Look at me. I'm just a secretary. Yet I'm the Chosen One.' She almost added, 'Apparently', but stopped herself just in time. 'What do we know about this place, other than that Moses came here with some birds once?'

'It was named after the beloved sister of the king,' Raleigh told her. 'They say that she died young. Her name was Nadia.'

Nadine shivered. That sounded far too close for comfort. Had her father given her that name on purpose? Lance put his arm around her, as if to let her know that he understood.

'And you're happy for me to die young, are you?' Nadine turned on her father. 'In order to prove your point?'

'No, of course not. But everything that's happening has been foretold.'

'Her pyramid would be the biggest then,' Hardcastle chipped in. 'Beloved sister and all that.'

'No,' Lance and Nadine said together.

'Kings born afterwards would have no allegiance to her,' Lance explained. 'She was a princess but not a queen. Later kings might want their pyramids to overshadow all the others, so each one would be built that bit bigger than the last. We're looking at the first royal family to live here and name this area.'

'Smaller, older tombs,' Nadine said. She walked to where there are smaller tombs, including one pyramid that was in almost perfect condition. It was as if time had stood still around it, so it avoided erosion and the storms that battered the desert. There was a more logical explanation and Nadine guessed that was to do with the people hidden behind a sand dune about a mile away.

'That's no good,' Hardcastle scoffed.

'It's a new one. Probably some rich Arab, wanting to die like the Pharaohs.'

'I don't think so,' Nadine replied. 'It's just been maintained by the Keepers of the Keys. It was obvious, really. I don't know why you didn't think of it, Mr. Hardcastle.'

Lance grinned. 'That's what happens when you send an arms dealer to do an archaeologist's job.'

'I'm only a secretary, and I noticed.'

'You're special.'

'I'm not,' she protested.

'You are special to me.'

'Oh, well, that's different.'

'Can we stop the lovey-dovey stuff and get into that tomb?' Hardcastle snapped.

Nadine walked up to the entrance and brushed sand off the door. As she did so, four keyholes became visible running vertically down the side of the door. 'There must be a system,' she said, looking at the keys in her hand. 'I don't know what will happen if I get it wrong, so be ready, everyone.'

The German soldiers had stopped what they were doing and stood around watching. Nadine was acutely aware of the machine guns they held. One wrong move and there could be a deadly firefight. But she had no way of knowing what was going to happen. She slipped her free hand into Lance's and he squeezed it tightly. As long as he was with her, she could do anything.

She put the keys in the locks in ascending order of the virtues as she had discovered them: Prudence, Justice, Temperance and Fortitude. As she placed the final key, the door swung open as if propelled from the inside. It was dark within, and she guessed there was yet another chamber.

'We need a torch,' she said, and one was put into her hand immediately. It felt odd to be in charge, but she knew that it was only momentary. As soon as Hardcastle and her father saw the jewel, it would be a question of which of them turned on her first.

As luck would have it, there was not

enough room in the chamber for anyone but Nadine, Lance, Raleigh Middleton and Hardcastle. That at least left the Germans outside.

The chamber was empty, apart from a sarcophagus lying up against a wall. It was tiny, no more than three feet high. It occurred to Nadine that if it was Nadia's grave, she had been very young indeed when she died, even allowing that people were not as tall in the past. That made her sad. Had she died protecting the stone? Would the same happen to Nadine?

She took a deep breath and opened the sarcophagus. There was an ancient figure swathed in bandages, and in its hands was a leather pouch. 'This is wrong,' said Nadine. 'It's grave robbing.'

Hardcastle had no such qualms. He snatched the pouch from the dead body's hands. As he did so, there was a faint rumble beneath them. Or was it above them? Inside the chamber it was difficult to tell.

'We need to get out,' Lance whispered. Nadine nodded. Hardcastle was already on his way, closely followed by Raleigh Middleton.

'Let me see,' Raleigh said. 'You promised me!'

'Hold your horses,' Hardcastle snapped. 'Men . . . shoot them as they — ' Hardcastle stopped mid-sentence.

When Nadine and Lance came out of the tomb they saw why. The prince, Mustafa and the others had somehow managed to creep up and disarm all the German soldiers. The Germans were sat in small groups with their hands on their heads and their own guns pointed at them. The prince himself had a gun pointed straight at Hardcastle.

'I just want to see it,' he said, in the same whining tone that Raleigh had used. 'Please.'

He opened the pouch, and as he did so, there was another rumble. Hardcastle ignored that and pulled out the jewel. Even Nadine could not resist looking. A sparkling sapphire of the very deepest blue, it was every bit as beautiful as she had been told.

But, as they looked on, a storm seemed to originate from the stone itself: starting off tiny, and just fitting into Hardcastle's hand, before it grew upwards into a spout, not unlike a tornado, battering everything around it and whipping up sand so that their way was blocked.

Somehow, amongst all the sand, images appeared. Some wonderful, some dreadful.

'Everyone, shut your eyes now!' she called. She snatched the jewel from Hardcastle. 'Shut your eyes.' Hardcastle fell to his knees, watching the images in the storm with growing horror. Nadine wondered if he saw what she saw, or whether he only saw his own future. Her father also fell to his knees, but he looked on in wonder. The prince and his people all obeyed Nadine, but the German soldiers looked on.

Nadine looked around and saw a young girl amidst the storm. For a moment it seemed that Nadine and the girl were one and the same, looking at each other across time, both understanding the enormity of what was happening. The girl covered her eyes, and suddenly Nadine knew what she had to do.

She turned to Lance, who was as resistant as everyone else, and reached up and kissed him hard on the mouth. Then he shut his eyes, clinging to her. As they kissed, everything within a few feet of them became calm. Only on the outside did the storm rage on. 'Don't look. Don't look,' Nadine whispered against his lips. 'It will destroy you. Do you understand?'

'Yes,' Lance said, his eyes clamped shut. 'Yes, I understand. But we could use it, honey, to do good. All the things we've seen so far, we can stop.'

'No, that will never happen. You know that. It will corrupt us just as it's corrupted them. We'll think we know better than everyone else and that makes us just as bad as the Hitlers of this world. Please, Lance, trust me and let it go.'

He nodded and she kissed him again.

Nadine turned to face the storm, still clinging to Lance. Her own eyelids were clamped shut, but she knew she would have to open them to do what needed to be done.

She opened her eyes and pulled her hand back. She had never been much good at rounders or netball at school — or at anything else, for that matter — but she needed to be good now. She hurled the stone into the raging sand storm, sending it as far as she possibly could. It was carried up by a gust of wind, gaining momentum, before spinning into the tornado and disappearing.

Nadine turned back and hid her face in Lance's neck. 'I love you,' she said.

'I love you too, Nadine.'

The storm raged around them, but they were both calm and content in their love for each other. Nothing else mattered.

16

Dear Aunt Clementine,

I am sorry that you're disappointed in me for not returning the Eye of the Storm to Britain. I made a decision based on what I had seen that no one should have that much power. If you are unhappy about it, then you should consider why you sent me. I assume that you knew the truth about me being the so-called Chosen One. Did it not occur to you that I was chosen because I would make the right decision? For what it's worth, Count Chlomsky agreed with me. Oh, yes, I know you had him spying on me, just as I was spying on others.

Mr. Hardcastle has gone quite mad since the events in the desert. He is under arrest, but has tried to escape several times to go back and look for the stone. I doubt he will find it.

We are told that all the German soldiers have deserted. Some were arrested in Cairo, and say they are happy to be imprisoned. They don't try to escape. I know why, because I saw much of what they saw in the sands.

My father likes to pretend that he knew all this would happen, but I find it hard to forgive him. I know I should, because family will be everything in the dark days to come, but I think of the pain he caused my mother and how he used her and it is hard.

I hope you will at least be happy to know that Lance and I are now married. We married as soon as we returned to Cairo. Our wedding was attended by the Count and Countess and by our friends Prince Ari and Princess Valerie, Mustafa and his daughter Akilah, and Mr. and Mrs. Barclay (nee Sutton). It was a ceremony full of joy and friendship.

Depending on what you want to believe of the story I have told you, I have either thrown the Eye of the Storm into the depths of time, or it is buried under billions of tons of shifting sands in the middle of the desert. Either way it will be a long time before it is found again.

My father said that love was not important, but he was wrong. My mother's love for me kept me safe for many years. I know that Lance and I will be separated for much of the duration of the war, as we both do our duty to our countries, but our love is what will sustain us all through the dark days to come. The love of a brother for his sister is what kept us safe in the desert and our love is what will keep us safe in the future. Love is the calm at the centre of the storm. Love is the fifth virtue . . .

Your loving niece,
Nadine Middleton-Smith.

P.S. One thing I *can* reveal, which I trust will give you hope, is that Uncle Winston will be just the man to lead us all through the coming storm. The people will have faith in him just as you always have.

We do hope that you have enjoyed reading this large print book.

Did you know that all of our titles are available for purchase?

We publish a wide range of high quality large print books including:
Romances, Mysteries, Classics
General Fiction
Non Fiction and Westerns

Special interest titles available in large print are:
The Little Oxford Dictionary
Music Book, Song Book
Hymn Book, Service Book

Also available from us courtesy of Oxford University Press:
Young Readers' Dictionary
(large print edition)
Young Readers' Thesaurus
(large print edition)

For further information or a free brochure, please contact us at:
Ulverscroft Large Print Books Ltd.,
The Green, Bradgate Road, Anstey,
Leicester, LE7 7FU, England.
Tel: (00 44) 0116 236 4325
Fax: (00 44) 0116 234 0205

Other titles in the
Linford Romance Library:

CHRISTMAS IN MELTDOWN

Jill Barry

When her assistant suddenly quits, struggling bistro owner Lucy is filled with despair. Top chef James rides to the rescue — but Lucy fears he's hijacking her menus. As electricity fizzes between the two, and festive delights fly from the kitchen, Lucy faces a business dilemma. Does James hold the key to success? Snow poses fresh challenges as each cook falls more deeply in love with the other. Will it be James or Lucy who melts first?

IN PERFECT HARMONY

Wendy Kremer

When Holly Watson starts work as a PA to music director Ian Travers, she's hoping for a simple part-time job to earn a little extra. She gets more than she bargained for, however — her new boss stirs decidedly unprofessional feelings within her. But she's not the only one so affected: Olivia de Noiret, a beautiful and sophisticated prima donna soprano, also has her eyes on Ian — and makes it very clear to Holly that she's already staked her claim . . .

CHRISTMAS IN THE BAY

Jo Bartlett

Maddie Jones runs a bookshop in the beautiful St Nicholas Bay. Devoted to her business, she's forgotten what it's like to have a romantic life — until Ben Cartwright arrives, and reminds her of what she's missing. But Ben isn't being entirely honest about what brings him to town — and when his professional ambition threatens Maddie's livelihood, their relationship seems doomed. When a flash flood descends on the Bay, all the community must pull together — will Ben stay or go?